COUNTRY BOYS

COUNTRY BOYS

WILD GAY EROTICA

EDITED BY
RICHARD LABONTÉ

CLEIS
PRESS

Cleis Press Inc., P.O. Box 14697, San Francisco, California 94114

Printed in the United States.
Cover design: Scott Idleman
Cover photograph: Superstock
Text design: Frank Wiedemann
Cleis logo art: Juana Alicia
First Edition.
10 9 8 7 6 5 4 3 2 1

For Asa, learning to be a country boy
For Percy, 1995–2006. Pretty boy.

Contents

| INTRODUCTION

When I moved to the country, after more than twenty years of big-city gay-ghetto life, primarily in Los Angeles and San Francisco, with extended stays in New York City, many of my friends were aghast. Could I cope with the absence of queer input? Could I even be openly gay?

Piffle. It's easy to be a country boy. I live mostly in a small town, population six thousand, and it's no secret that I'm queer. The bank tellers (all three of them) know it—they added my husband Asa to my bank account, using our wedding certificate as documentation. The owner of the best bakery in town knows it—she provided our wedding cake. The people at the post office (inside the downtown drugstore) know it—after all, they handle the mail addressed to *"Books to Watch Out For/Gay Men's Edition"* and "Submissions/*Best Gay Erotica.*" All my neighbors, nosy or not, know it—they've seen Asa and I walking our dogs, young Zak and elder Percy (who passed away in the fall of 2006 after thirteen years), looking like any comfy gay couple, though we certainly don't dress alike. And we're not the only queers in town. Heck, we're not the only queers on the block. One gay couple runs a B&B two doors to the east, another gay couple runs another B&B a block to the west, and yet another gay couple—together for thirty-five years—are renovating a home, preparing to move in soon. Beyond that, a community of homo-friends hang out in a curve-in-the-road hamlet about twenty minutes from our front door (running a small farmer's market, providing local computer sales and service) not far from country land that hosts radical faerie gatherings throughout the year. And of course, gaydar works even here—I stay home and read and write most days, but Asa has met several fellow travelers—including the fag hairdresser all the blue-haired ladies adore—in our wee town's one good coffee shop.

When we're not in town, we're on a two-hundred-acre farm about forty-five minutes away—population whoever is there at the time; the nearest two year-round neighbors live down the road and out of sight, a ten-minute walk from our farmhouse. But the father and son who hay our fields and deliver our firewood know I'm gay—they've seen Asa and I walking through those fields, hand in hand. The handyman who comes by every so often to fix this and that knows I'm gay—he's had long talks with Asa about living with AIDS. The woman who runs the village library, where I go to check email when I'm at the farm, knows I'm gay—she always asks after Asa when I come in. And I'm pretty sure the women who work the register at the convenience store/gas station in the village, the only place to go for forgotten breakfast milk and eggs, and sweet fresh corn in season, know I'm gay—they adore Asa, and ask after me when he gasses up our truck or goes in for a loaf of warm store-baked rye bread or oatmeal cookies. And we're not the only queers in the county, either: two of our best friends, a lesbian couple, live in the closest small town to the farm.

No question: rural living can be as queer as you want it to be.

This collection reflects that reality—except, perhaps, that there are none of Vincent Diamond's alligators hereabouts, and our county fair lacks Michael Bracken's rodeo riders (though I chatted with an out-of-town gay couple at last year's annual Maple Sugar Festival), and Dominic Santi's Native American reservation has no equivalent, and Shane Allison's redneck South is an alien mindset where I live, and we're far away in time and place from Dale Chase's nineteenth-century wagon-train romance.

But I imagine, sadly, that some young man, a man neither Asa nor I has yet met here in our patch of rural Eastern Ontario, could well find himself mirrored in the closeted uncertainty, even pain, of Jay Neal's high school students with dusty Kansas town secrets, of Wayne Courtois' young men and their isolated farm encounter, of Steve Berman's fated farm boy and his fantastical partners, or of Simon Sheppard's boyhood pals and their missed opportunity; others, more lucky, may have already exulted in the exuberant sexual satisfaction of Jack Fritscher's lusty birthday boy or of Kal Cobalt's lonely diner proprietor (hey: there are a couple of diners in our town).

And I'd like to think that, somewhere in the woods and fields minutes away from my apartment's front door, or surrounding my farm, other young men are savoring the satiation and sexual self-discovery celebrated by C. B. Potts' woodland poacher, J. M. Snyder's county-fair farm boy, Karl Taggart's well-tooled handyman, Duane Williams' summer-hire field hand, or Tom Cardamone's pastoral river boy.

We are everywhere, boys, even in the country.

Richard Labonté
Perth/Calabogie, Ontario

LAYING BY

Dale Chase

We were well on to California that summer of 1846 before I truly knew what was upon me. Crossing rivers and valleys astride a well-worn mule, I came to maturity in new territory, reaching my twenty-first year the day we rafted the wagons across the Platte and set out onto the Great Plain. Being of an observant nature, I also began to see things among men that were before unknown to me.

Captain Virgil Dawe and his cohort Jim Frazer led fifty wagons, buggies, carts and other wheeled contraptions through the best and worst of it, and I thought highly of them, knowing they'd successfully made the crossing many times before. Then one night when darkness had cooled the day's heat and people slept inside tents scattered along the bank of the Sweetwater, I ventured late to the river's edge and there in the light of a half moon saw Dawe and Frazer standing naked in knee-high water, Dawe with his cock up Frazer's bottom, going at him. Though stunned at such a sight, I did not turn away because my own prick came up hard and I will confess I got it out and began to pull on it, the sight stirring my juices as never before.

Dawe held Frazer at the hips and went faster and faster, then threw his head back as if to roar but let out not a sound and I knew he was spurting into the man's bottom because I was at that very moment doing the same onto the ground before me.

When I had spent but still stood, dick in hand, I watched the two men finish, at which Dawe withdrew and I saw his big thing. He then turned Frazer to him and they pressed together, writhed some, then Dawe dropped down and took his cohort's cock into his mouth. My own stirred at such a sight and as I held it I knew myself more untried than before, reaching manhood with little knowledge of the way of things. Watching Dawe's head bob on the prick, I considered having my mouth on one, the fat knob against my tongue, the rod's stiffness, but then I saw Frazer buck and Dawe pulled off, took the cock in hand and pumped as it let go a stream of spunk. Frazer was much agitated throughout, settling only when empty. Then Dawe stood and embraced his friend.

As I was hidden in brush, I stayed put and saw them leave the water, dress on the shore and head toward camp as if they'd done no more than bathe. Shaken by all this, I stripped and slid into the cool water where I thought of them going at it which got my dick up again.

I considered how we had traveled nearly a month, Frazer driving the wagon for Dawe, the Captain on horseback, and I considered them fucking—because that's what it was even though I'd understood a fuck to be man and woman—up the bottom. I tried to imagine a cock in me and this gave me such a pleasurable jolt that I righted myself in the shallow, squatted and put a finger up myself, thinking of Dawe in me. This aroused me so much I worked my prick and soon set gobs of stuff to floating

on the water. From then all was changed. I felt my years in a new
way as I'd seen the true nature of man.

I began to watch other men as never before, aware now
when two talked quietly off to one side. Before I'd thought they
discussed the journey and maybe they did and I was pushing
things onto them they didn't want but sometimes they'd go into
a wagon or tent and there would be quiet and I'd see nobody
noticed, others went on about their business, but I listened when
I could, heard things, grunts and such, and I'd get hard because
I knew it was a fuck.

It was common knowledge men fucked their way across the
country because babies were born as a result, women sprouting
full along the way, and there were fights at times as we were
very much a town on wheels with all the hurts and jealousies of
a town fixed in place. But now I saw there was more to it and I
wondered if others noticed what I did. Sometimes it was nothing but a man with his cock out, pissing, but sometimes there
was no piss and, thinking himself unseen, he worked the thing
and spurted. Dawe went at Frazer regular and when they slept
in their tent, I'd take up a place outside that was close by and
hear them fuck.

I traveled with my pa, an uncle and aunt, and several cousins,
tending our small band of cattle, helping the family out when
needed. Some days after I'd seen what I'd seen, I rode along
thinking on it because I could think of nothing else. It wasn't
that I was ignorant of life. I'd seen bulls mount cows, seen men
naked, hired hands pissing in the open and sometimes keeping a
hand on their dicks longer than needed. And I'd heard Ma and
Pa at night as their bedroom was next to mine, heard the fucking, and I considered that now—forgive me Ma—him putting it
in her where it was meant. But Dawe had no woman and I wondered was that it? Absent a wife, did a man fuck his friend?

Dawe rode up beside me one day as I thought such things and I could not speak because it felt as if I'd been caught with my hand in my pants. He was passing down the line to tell us we'd stop early as Mrs. Wynn would deliver her baby directly.

"How old are you, boy?" he asked out of nowhere and I told him I'd turned twenty-one at the Platte's South Fork.

"Man now," he declared and he held my gaze so long I wondered if he knew I'd seen him fuck. He was a rough man but handsome, thirty-six I'd learned. Tall and thick with dark hair that curled at his neck, he had a welcome smile and showed it then and I knew he would, if I wanted, fuck me. My cock was hard and I think he knew this but he kept to business, asked me to ride down the line to tell the others we were stopping for the day.

By now the wagons were well separated so it took some time to spread the word. Once I'd done the task, the first wagons were already stopped and by late afternoon we had settled into a fine spot along the river. As Mrs. Wynn was delivered of a fine boy, I thought of telling Dawe he could fuck me, I was ready, but he was in conversation with several men, Frazer among them, and I knew his cohort would that day get the cock.

I busied myself helping Pa and Uncle Ned with the stock, then went out with two cousins to hunt antelope which was a failure. We had a fine meal that evening anyway after which Sam Harkin got out his fiddle and there came singing and dancing. The night was clear, a bit cooler which was a relief after the day's heat, and as others enjoyed the music I went off behind the wagon, got out my prick and hardly pulled before I sprayed my spunk. Once empty I leaned against the wagon and thought of Dawe some more, knew he'd put it up Frazer that night. With my dick still in hand I pictured him mounting his friend as a bull would his cow, going at him like before, and soon my cock was up again and I had myself another good pull.

We followed the Platte's North Fork for over a week through grasslands where the stock took little notice the green had gone brown. It was easy travel, the way wide ahead, buffalo plentiful. I watched Dawe and he watched me and I wondered how I could tell him I'd fuck but then we reached Chimney Rock and everything changed.

I'd heard about this great stone formation sticking up in the middle of nowhere as it was a marker for all westward travel, a pyramid topped by what appeared a factory chimney. We camped within sight of it and everyone remarked on the landmark, how it did look like a chimney, rough hewn but tall, jutting out from the hill at its base. I, of course, in my awakened state, saw it otherwise. From first sight it appeared to me an erect cock and try as I might, I could not dispel this image. In fact, when we were settled, tents up, fires lit, I rode out to it with the cousins and looked up at the thing, thinking again of a man lying with his prick up that way and doing something about it. I felt ready to burst with need and when the cousins rode back to camp, I stayed on at the rock and while astride my mule got out my prick and had myself a go.

I was thus in a state of near constant arousal—not an unpleasant state in which to reside—when a party of men on horseback leading two pack mules rode into camp. They were ten in number, said they were headed to California and might they camp with us for the night. Dawe and others welcomed them and later, after supper, we all sat together and they told us their story.

The most outspoken of the lot was about my age, a sandy-haired Kentuckian name of Luke Healy who said it was his third crossing and he was destined to make many more because he liked the adventure. Said early on he'd read stories about the West by Fenimore Cooper and on that had undertaken his first trip and was not disappointed. He'd learned much in his travels, knew all about the Indians and had met the famed scout Caleb Greenwood who told of California. "Sutter offers six sections of his Spanish grant land to families who settle near his fort," he said, adding that this was a good reason to choose California over Oregon. This provoked much discussion as we had yet to reach the fork where the Oregon route split from that to California. Luke sat next to me and I became most interested in him as he spoke easy and well and was given to good humor. Then later, when people turned in, he and I sat together and talked. As I'd told him my name before, he began that way.

"Cullen, tell me about yourself."

"There's no adventure in my life," I offered. "I travel with my Pa, an uncle and aunt and three cousins. We farmed in Illinois, then my Ma died and Pa wanted to come west."

"Then you've begun your adventure," he said. "There's much ahead and not so easy as this."

We sat in silence a bit, then I asked how he'd come to ride with the other men.

"They have no families and are young like me, eager to see new territory but none want the burden of a wagon. Six of us met up in St. Joseph, then were joined at the Kansas River by four who'd set out from Independence."

I thought about the party of men, wondered if they got up to things. Knowing what I did, it seemed it would happen regular and I longed to know this but couldn't see how to ask. All I could say was, "How do you all get along?"

"There are disputes on occasion just as with your party but we are fine for the most part. I was elected captain as I have the most experience."

"Tell me about what lies ahead," I said, not able to ask about fucking.

"Fort Laramie is not far and that's usually a couple days laying by but then come the Black Hills, rougher going, and more
river crossings. Independence Rock then, you've heard of that,
and once past it you go through the South Pass of the Rocky
Mountains. After that there's Fort Hall, some hard country, a
long stretch along the Humboldt River, then the forty-mile desert which some say is the worst but others say it's crossing the
Sierra Nevada. But once over that, you're in the Sacramento
Valley and Sutter's Fort."

I asked questions about each spot, not because I wanted to
know but because I wanted more of Luke and with his telling I
gained the sound of him and the way he told, capturing his spirit
in my own way. He related his first time, hooking up with an
old scout who'd made the crossing in 1841 which nearly failed,
many wagons abandoned along the way.

We talked well into the night and stopped only because Pa
came and got me, told me to get some sleep. It surprised me that
I didn't want to leave Luke's side and he saw this and said we'd
meet in the morning.

"Are you riding on tomorrow?" I asked, an ache filling me.

"Don't know," he answered which I read as reluctance but in
my gut—or maybe my dick—I knew I suffered wishful thinking.
I slept outside that night, away from the others. In the moonlight Chimney Rock stood a dark erection and I abused my cock
something fierce, finding I now thought not of Dawe but of
Luke.

At dawn I awoke painfully hard and had an earnest go at myself as the camp awakened. I had just spurted when I found Luke
standing over me. He passed a look that told me he knew what
I'd done and that he too had begun the day thusly. "I'm headed
to the river to wash," he said and I knew he meant me to join
him which I did. He stripped off his shirt and I saw he wore no

undershirt, chest bare with more of his sandy hair spread across a fine frame. Wading into the water, he proceeded to splash and rub himself and my prick stirred with the sight as he lingered at his man tits, rubbing the things. I tried not to fix on him, began to wash my own scrawny chest, but I could not keep from looking. The hair ran down his stomach and disappeared into his pants where I knew it sprouted full between his legs and how I wished he'd drop his drawers and wash his cock so I could see. He finished up with water over his head and shook it out like a dog, then came up grinning. "Next stop, I'm having me a bath," he declared with a smile.

When he went to join his party I thought him lost and wondered if that was the way of westward travel, meeting up with folks and losing them along the way, but then Luke came back over to me and said he would ask Dawe if he might leave his party and join ours as his was short on food. "And sense," he added before he went to find Dawe.

We broke camp and began the day's travel north toward Fort Laramie, alongside the North Platte, and I found myself in high spirits to such an extent that Pa remarked on it and I had to say it was due to the fine summer day and easy progress.

As I was herding stock later on and lost in thoughts of fucking which never really left my mind now, Luke rode up beside me which only made it worse. He had a fine black horse that made my mule look even more ragged and he sat astride his mount like he was captain of the whole country. "Dawe welcomed me into your party," he said. "Told me I could help scout, tend the cattle." I grinned, embarrassed that I was so happy and so aroused.

Pa liked Luke but then everyone did. He was attentive to all, polite with the elders, amusing to the children, helpful to the women. And when we neared Scott's Bluff, a huge rock formation that would block our route and force us south to Robidoux Pass, he suggested we ride out to the bluff and have a look around. I was near beside myself as we would for the first time be truly alone.

Those in camp had settled into singing and dancing to old Harkin's fiddle and we heard his music for some time as we rode away. As it was mid-June, the day was long and we enjoyed an easy ride to the bluff which Luke said was our own Gibraltar, which puzzled me until he told of the giant rock across the ocean.

"How do you know such things?" I asked as we climbed off our mounts.

"Books," he said. "My Ma taught me to read early and she liked books and encouraged me to do the same."

I didn't know what to do next but Luke did. He sat in a patch of grass and took off his boots and socks, acting like resting his feet was his purpose. "C'mon, Cullen," he said and I joined him. We were so far from camp we would not be seen and so I settled into the tall grass and bared my feet. Luke then lay back, put hands under his head as pillow, drew a long breath and let it out and I did likewise, stretching out beside him. Of course my dick was hard and I thought how even his bared feet had aroused me because they led to his legs which between them held what I wanted most.

He said nothing and I wondered if it was up to me to see to things even as I wasn't sure what things were. Maybe he just meant to rest here with a friend; maybe he just wanted clear of the others for a while; but maybe he wanted to fuck. Why else bring me out here with him?

Before I knew it my hand had strayed to my crotch and I rubbed myself as I spoke. My words came with difficulty but I knew if I didn't say it now it would never get said.

"You're a man of the world," I began which caused Luke to snort a laugh. "Well, compared to me you are," I amended and he agreed.

"Anyway," I continued, then stopped, for how was I to say it?

"What?" Luke asked.

"I am curious," I said, "but I have no one I can ask so will ask you."

"Then ask."

"I saw Dawe fucking Frazer some time back, at the river's edge, putting his dick up his friend's bottom, and since then I've heard them going at it regular so I want to know is this what men do because I never knew of it before."

My hand was still on my cock, clutching it in fear I'd done wrong in saying what I'd said. He'd either answer me or fight me.

"It's what men do," he said quietly. It was the softest he'd yet spoken and I heard him sincere and caring in even those few words, which allowed me to press on.

"I am curious about the men in your party, traveling without women. Did you fuck among you?"

"A man fucks when he needs it," Luke said, "just like the stock. Fuck who's available. We did it as we needed. Climb onto a man in the night; most are willing to take a cock. One night a man name of Ethan and me were guarding the horses and he just got it out and we did it there standing. It's everywhere, Cullen. I've seen it everywhere."

"Tell me."

Here he undid his pants and pushed them down to reveal a good-sized and very hard prick which he took in hand as he spoke. I hurried to get mine out as I listened.

"I once saw a scout with his buckskins at his ankles, fucking a naked furry mountain man who looked more bear than man. And one man who traveled with a wife put it to his hired man more than her. At Fort Hall I came upon a man with it in another, going at it, and they saw me and didn't care I watched and when they finished they asked did I want it."

"And did you?"

"I put it up one, then the other, and allowed them the same of me."

Spurts shot out of my dick because his talk had pushed me over. I pumped frantically, crying out and carrying on and not caring who heard or saw. Luke then turned to me, ran a finger through the spunk on my belly. "Have you ever fucked?" he asked.

I couldn't speak. A rush filled me, a flood of words and feelings, everything that had piled up since I'd first seen Dawe doing it to Frazer, and I wanted to let it all go now, tell Luke everything, but all I did was shake my head.

"But you want to."

I shuddered with pleasure at the thought, then nodded at which he stood up and pulled off his pants and didn't stop there. He made a bed of sorts of his clothes and had me strip as well and we lay on our shirts and pants and he ran his hands over me and invited me to explore him as well. His thing was so ready it was wet at the tip.

"Give it a pull," he told me and I put a hand to him which caused all manner of excitement in me. He began to move in my palm, to push and as he did he took hold of my cock and did likewise and we lay facing one another, working prick for a bit. "You can suck it as well," he said and I told him I knew this as Dawe had sucked Frazer.

"Go ahead if you want," he told me and I saw he was encouraging it so I slid down and touched his knob with my tongue which caused even more unrest in me and I fixed on the thing and began a fierce suck until Luke pushed me off. "Keep that up and you'll have spunk in your throat," he said. "Better we fuck."

This took some doing. Luke first wet a finger with spit and put it up my bottom. I had my back to him now, lying on my side, cock in hand. Over and over he ran spit into me and each time worked my hole, telling me to relax, make it easy, that I had to open up.

I was getting agitated with him doing this to me and finally couldn't hold back, gave myself a fast pull and squirted my stuff, which was better than ever due to his finger working my backside. He continued at this but finally said he could wait no longer, he had to fuck.

Now he put me onto all fours to mount me from behind. "I'll wet my prick," he said, "but it'll still hurt like hell but you just bear it and there'll be pleasure." And he got in behind and put his hands on my butt to open me and then I felt his cock at my hole, pushing. "Open up," he said over and over. "Let it in."

He pushed and it hurt some and I tried not to fight it and then he lost patience and shoved hard and popped in. I cried out but then he had the whole thing in me and I found I liked that.

"You'll like this more," he said when I told him how it felt and he pulled back but not out, then went in again and we were soon in a full-out fuck, him going at me like some animal with grunts and growls as he did it, slapping my bottom and then he shouted, "It's here, oh Jesus, it's here!" and his grunt became muffled and he thrust hard as he let go in me and I found myself in a new world, taking a man's spunk.

He rode me a good bit, filling my passage with his stuff, and then he was done and pulled out and fell over onto his back. I turned round to see his cock gone soft, some of his spunk still at the tip. I reached over and ran a finger through it.

Darkness soon came but we stayed in our little bed, not caring about the mosquitoes' interest in our bare skin. We played with one another, feeling and prodding and Luke telling me more what he'd done with men and what he'd do with me. Finally, when we were both hard again, he said I could fuck his bottom. "If you want," he added.

I had come a thousand times but always in hand. Now I could gain release inside another and more, inside someone I was caring for. When I didn't quickly reply, lost in thought of doing it to him, he reached for my dick, gave it a tug and said, "Fuck me, Cullen." And then he got onto all fours and there was his bottom for me to use. I wet my prick as had he and I ran gobs of spit into him, then held him open and pushed in which caused my breath to catch, such was the feel.

Luke moaned beneath me and said it again, "Fuck me," and I began to do it, to shove into him, in and out, and my juice came quickly and I spurted long before I wanted to. As I came I rode him hard for it felt much like I was astride some animal, him being my pony now, but finally I emptied and fell back, cock gone soft. Luke turned and sat, put an arm around me and I thought he'd say something then but he didn't. After a bit more he said we'd best get back to camp.

From then on we fucked every day, sometimes twice, sometimes riding away from camp or ahead to scout water and grass. We mostly slept outside, next to one another, and when the others were asleep we'd get into each other, fuck and fuck and fuck. I had never been so happy.

Of course it wasn't all play and Luke was right about rough travel ahead. Riding alongside the Platte had been the easy part but once we'd crossed it the final time and hit what Luke called the real West where it was dry and barren, it was rough going and axles broke and oxen died and people too. There came relief at Fort Hall and sometimes at streams we'd find pockets of

cottonwoods out on the plain and we'd camp and fill our water
barrels for the next leg of the journey.

Luke was beloved by all as he proved to be easygoing while
competent with any task. He did whatever Dawe asked and I
noted Dawe saw us together often and I thought he'd come to
know our bond was as his with Frazer.

We saw Independence Rock where settlers had marked their
names, big whale of a thing plopped down on the prairie, and
while others viewed the landmark, Luke and I rode around the
other side and fucked in its shadow. Then came the South Pass
through the Rockies which was not a bad pull as it's a slow
grade but after that it was like Luke said and then came the forty-mile desert which was true hardship. We pushed through the
whole of it in one day, stopping only to rest the stock a couple
times for there was no water or grass, and Mrs. Wynn's baby
died partway and we buried him. But we reached the Truckee
River with the Sierra Nevada ahead, looking like a granite wall
but none cared for they were happy to be past the desert and
have water and grass.

It was while laying by here for a week of rest before the next
hard leg, crossing the Sierra, that Luke and I came to our under-
standing though this was not much easier than a desert crossing
or climbing over a mountain.

While we had fucked regular and clung to one another at
such moments, he would then hurry away and I came to wonder
what this meant because later on he'd be his old self and would
give me the eye that said he wanted it again.

People were tired at the Truckee, months piling up and making them ragged, short in temper. The cattle had near stampeded
when they first caught smell of grass and wagons were in need of
repair as were some people but after a few days all were rested
and looking to the end of the trip.

Luke volunteered to ride ahead and scout the South Pass to make certain it remained clear and Dawe agreed. Luke asked me to ride along which I knew meant to fuck so I went but as we neared the place where we would cross to our final destination, I suffered a sense of loss even though no loss had yet come. I saw how Luke would reach Sutter's Fort and turn and head east in his pursuit of adventure and it pained me to see myself taking up a life without him. It was near October now, our time together running out, so I spoke as I never would have imagined I could.

We'd stopped at the bottom of the pass and it was easy to see it remained clear and there had been no need to come ahead so I knew it was just to fuck but Luke made no such move like he usually did, finding us a spot even if just to do it standing at a tree with my pants down. And I knew we had now come to something, much as had the wagon train, a last obstacle before starting the new life. But how to say it? I knew only I didn't want him to leave me and had no idea if that meant he should stay in California or I should go adventuring with him. I was not a man of words as Luke was and I sat on my poor tired mule wishing Luke would speak what I knew. But all he said was, "It's hell to get the wagons through," and I wanted to say I didn't care about wagons or anything else and could we fuck because I needed him too many ways and that was the only way open to me as yet. Finally I managed to get something out. "But once through, it's easy going."

"You've still got Bear Valley which ain't bad," he said, "but there's a rough stretch after that, still some high ridges and forest before you get down to the Sacramento Valley."

"And what then, Luke?"

He gave no answer, at least not one spoken. Instead he got off his horse and made me dismount the mule and he led me where there was some cover and made ready to fuck me but I wouldn't, even when he had his cock out, even when I wanted it.

"Are you going east again?" I asked, near choking on the words because they made it possible which I couldn't bear. "Are you going to leave me?"

"No," he said and I wanted more than that but he was pulling at my pants and so I dropped them and bent and took his cock and he was rough, angry even as he took his pleasure, and my cock stayed soft, cowed by feelings churning my gut. When Luke came he let out a yell like he'd been knifed or shot and as I took his stuff I feared it was the last time because he'd given me one word and it wasn't enough to build on. Then he was done and pulled out and I stood with pants down, not caring I was bare like that and him with his dick out and we stood apart and I tried not to cry.

"I don't understand," I said, choking up.

"I don't neither," he said which surprised me as he was the man of experience and always had answers.

"What's between us..." I started but stopped because that wasn't it because that was speaking for him too and I couldn't do that so I tried again. "I have come to feel for you, Luke," I said but couldn't keep my eyes on him as it didn't sound right even though true. But when he gave no reply it turned the lock in me and it all rushed out because what did it matter now if I was to lose him anyway?

"I don't know what's right anymore but I know how I feel and I want to be with you, Luke, to make a life together, maybe farm or get a little spread with cattle. Get those six sections from Sutter. I can't take you leaving."

"I said I won't."

"You gave me one word and I need more. Tell me what's in your heart, Luke. I've told you what's in mine."

He put his cock away so I pulled up my pants and we stood

like a pair of gunslingers ready to shoot it out. But he finally told how it was with him. "This has never happened to me," he said, "feeling like I do and I don't know any more than you what's right. We're friends and we fuck and I want it to go on but more than that I can't tell."

"But you won't turn and go east."

"No, I won't."

"Because you want to stay with me."

He considered this and I saw it was foreign to him, like it didn't yet fit while I already wore it. For once I knew more so I led now. "It's all right then. When we get to Sutter's Fort we can decide where to go next. I don't have to stay with my Pa. He's fine with his brother and that family. I hear good things about San Francisco and we might find a life there. And who knows what lies ahead. California is the land of promise."

Speaking my piece gave me courage and I approached him, embraced him, put my lips to his and felt the whole of me grow warm. He stood stock-still awhile, then a hand found the small of my back, then the other my shoulder, and he pressed hard against me as the kiss went on. And there we stood in the shadow of the Sierra Nevada, grinding our bodies together while our pricks came up hard.

GOODLAND, KANSAS

Jay Neal

Alan met Donny for the first time at Ross's funeral, though he'd known for some time who he was: Donny was the *other* gay person in town.

For his part, Donny also knew who Alan was, and was hoping to meet him. He finally got his chance at the potluck reception following the service, behind Alan in the line at the buffet table.

"Those potatoes look really tasty," Donny said as Alan dipped a spoon into the casserole. Donny thought his remark particularly banal, but it got the conversation started.

"They are. My mom makes them. It's my Aunt Becky's recipe for 'funeral potatoes.'"

"I guess we've never been introduced—I'm Donny Doyle."

"Sure. I mean, I know who you are but we haven't. Been introduced, I mean. I'm Alan Morrison."

"It must have been quite a shock for you when Ross died."

Alan looked more thoughtful than sad. "I suppose it was a surprise, the accident and all, but..."

"I'm sorry. I thought you and he had been pretty close."

"Oh, we were, at least until the end of high school."

"What happened?"

Now Alan seemed more distracted. "Oh, that's a long story."

Donny barely hesitated to take his chance. "Maybe we could have a cup of coffee this week or something and you could tell me."

Alan seemed surprised by Donny's offer. "Yes. Yes, all right then. How about Wednesday at the diner. Ten-ish?"

"Sounds great. Ten-ish it is."

Alan smiled and nodded his head in a distracted way, then moved off to spend some time with Kenny, whom he had finally spotted. Donny watched and absently took his first bite of funeral potatoes.

Kenny was late for the meeting, but then Kenny was often late for the meetings. Eighth grade was off to a busy start for him, but it wasn't like he had all the after-school band rehearsals or theater projects like Alan, or all the after-school swim meets or debate-club practice that Ross had. It was all the after-school chores on his aunt and uncle's farm that kept him busy until late in the afternoon.

And then, of course, their farm would *have* to be clear on the other side of town from the clubhouse. And so Kenny always ended up bicycling across town as fast as he could, shooting down Caldwell Street then across Seventeenth Street and then across the railroad tracks and around behind the grain elevators on the west side of town. Invariably he arrived out of breath at their secret clubhouse: a shack in the woods behind the junkyard.

He dropped his bike on the ground and dashed inside, where he found Ross and Alan already sitting on the only furniture they had: a red bench seat from an old Pontiac. They were having one of their intellectual discussions.

"See," Ross said, "I don't think we're significant enough to be a major body part like the armpit. We're so crappy that we need to be something more like the pimple on the nose of the universe."

"I still think," Alan countered, "that 'asshole of the universe' would be perfectly acceptable."

"Nonsense! Kenny, what do you say? Resolved: That Goodland, Kansas, is such a disgusting and boring place to live that it is best described as the *blank* of the universe."

"Toe-jam," Kenny offered. Ross and Alan laughed and slapped their legs like this was the funniest thing, even though the response was predictable. *Toe-jam* was Kenny's favorite word, except maybe for *booger.*

"Toe-jam it is!" Ross intoned. "Goodland, Kansas, shall henceforth be known as the toe-jam of the universe!"

They all whooped some more with delight at this remarkable witticism. As they calmed down, Ross announced that it was time for the day's reading. He reached into his backpack and pulled out a glossy magazine, which he held up for inspection.

The cover showed two naked men in lurid, full color. At least, they looked naked, but it was difficult to be certain. One was holding a frying pan and bending over a stove. The other was standing right behind the first, real close to him. Their naked butts were both facing the camera. Strictly speaking, one was not entirely naked: he wore a tall, white chef's hat.

Alan read the title, "Sausage and Eggs." It was a change from their usual big-tit- and fat-assed-women magazines.

"Where do you get these?" Alan asked.

Ross answered with worldly insouciance. "From my dad's desk. He confiscates them in raids and keeps them there where he thinks they're safe and no one knows. Deputy Connor looks at them when Dad's out of the office—we pretend it's our little secret. My dad never notices."

The three sat in silence for a minute and contemplated the possible meaning of "Sausage and Eggs."

"But what are they doing?" Kenny asked at last.

"They're doing *it*," Alan explained.

"But they're guys." Kenny sounded confused.

"Sure, guys can do *it* too. Here, look." Ross flipped toward the back of the magazine. "See, you can see Mr. Chef's bone going right into the other guy's butt."

"Eeeuw! That's gross. What else do they do?"

Ross turned back to the beginning and proceeded more slowly through the pages. For the first time, they saw men kissing—with tongues in each other's mouth!—men licking each other's nipples, one man with his face buried up to his nose in another man's hairy ass, enormous hard-ons, men licking enormous hard-ons, enormous hard-ons in mouths, and enormous hard-ons in assholes displayed in several unusually athletic positions. All told, it was quite an educational experience.

Ross tossed the magazine toward his backpack, and slapped his hands on his legs. "Well," he said, "now it's time for the Sacred Ritual." As if on cue, all three stood, opened their belts, dropped their shorts, and sat back on the bench seat.

Kenny regarded his own hard-on critically, then compared it visually to those of his companions, noting that Ross's bush—he had been the first to grow pubic hair—was getting noticeably thicker. "Do you think they'll ever get bigger, like the ones in the magazine?"

"I'm sure they will, Kenny," Ross said, "except maybe for yours, which will probably always be two inches long."

Kenny scowled and Alan poked Ross in the ribs with his

elbow. Enough talk. On with the Sacred Ritual.

Ross had shown both the others basic jerk-off technique toward the end of seventh grade but in the few months since, they had each adopted personal methods. Ross preferred to make his hand slick with spit and rub his dick vigorously. Kenny used his thumb and two fingers just under the head of his dick. Alan liked to touch himself lightly first, inside his thighs and on his balls, and then use slow, steady strokes.

Regardless, none took very long to reach a dry climax. Mostly dry, that is. Sometime since the beginning of the current school year Ross had begun producing a few drops of cum. It would ooze from the slit in his dick, then he would touch it with his index finger and lift his hand slowly, seeing how far he could stretch the thread of semen before it broke. Alan and Kenny watched with focused attention and not a little envy. Today it must have stretched to nearly three inches.

Ross then said, in an overloud voice, "Now, the Sacred Flame. Kenny, do you have the torch?"

Kenny reached forward, rummaged in his shorts, and produced a butane lighter.

"Good," Ross said. "We can proceed." He stood up, turned smartly to face the bench seat, then squatted on it with his knees and leaned against the back.

"Ready the torch!" Kenny reached behind Ross's butt, flicked the lighter, and held the flame close to Ross's asshole.

"Here it—comes." Ross clenched his asshole tight so that his fart came out with a long, high-pitched whistle.

The fart ignited into a fine jet of flame shooting straight out of Ross's butt. It whistled down in pitch, then the flame died.

"Over five seconds, and it must have been at least twelve inches!" Alan said with evident delight.

Ross jumped off the bench, his still-hard dick bouncing in

front of him, and clapped his hands. "Excellent! Our meeting is now adjourned."

O'Rourke's Diner is an institution in Goodland. Granny O'Rourke has served breakfast daily to all the men who sit at the long table just inside the front door for about as long as any of them can remember.

Breakfast is served from six to nine. After that, Maeve O'Rourke, Granny O'Rourke's daughter-in-law, comes in to get ready for lunch, which starts at eleven. Betweentimes you can have coffee—in bottomless cups!—and a slice of pie if you're hungry. The justifiably famous pies are made by Maeve's sister Rose. Coconut cream is her specialty, but there is certainly nothing wrong with her apple pie. Her strawberry-rhubarb pie is seasonal and disappears fast.

When Donny got to the diner at a little past ten, he found Alan already in a booth toward the back. Two mugs of coffee and two slices of coconut cream pie were on the table.

"I went ahead and ordered the coconut cream. I hope that's okay with you."

"Always been my favorite. Thanks."

They sat silently for a bit while Donny was busy with putting creamer and sugar in his coffee, stirring it thoroughly, and taking a couple of appreciative bites of his pie.

"Well," Donny started hesitantly. "I know it's a bit weird making a date at a funeral...."

"Oh! This is a date then? Finally!"

"Finally?"

"You wouldn't believe the number of times I dreamed about having a date with the only other homo in town, trying to imagine what it would be like."

"And what did you imagine?"

"Oh, I don't think I know you well enough yet to reveal some of those intimate secrets. However, most were a bit more torrid than coffee and pie at O'Rourke's, that's for sure."

Donny was embarrassed so he changed the subject. "You'd known Ross for a long time, hadn't you?"

"Ever since third grade, when his family moved to town and Ross's father was made police chief."

"Did you know that everyone in the high school called you 'Friends of Dorothy'?"

"Really?"

Donny nodded. "Kenny was 'Scarecrow,' or just 'Crow.' "

"No doubt because he'd started growing and was so lanky. I imagine Ross was 'Tin Man.' "

"Right, and you were 'Dandy'..."

"...for 'Dandy Lion.' How prophetic."

"It was thought very clever at the time. I think it was because you three seemed to have something really special going."

"We did, I guess. Ninth grade was a great time, and the summer after was even better. We were inseparable and spent all our time together at the pool. I don't think we were ever as close again as we felt then. It was our endless summer and it seemed like we'd be best friends forever."

Goodland viewed its municipal swimming pool with understandable civic pride. It was built in 1936 by the Works Progress Administration. The pool had a capacity of 385,037 gallons, making it 37 gallons larger than the WPA pool built the same year in Holton, Kansas.

That same year Goodland built a new post office on Eleventh Street and a WPA artist named Kenneth Adams painted a mural he called *Rural Delivery*. Nineteen thirty-six was a good year for civic pride in Goodland.

When Ross and Alan and Kenny moved up to ninth grade at Goodland High School (Go Cowboys! Go Cowgirls!), Ross had already been swimming competitively for three years and winning trophies for the Goodland Municipal Pool Torpedoes. So it was no surprise when, that summer after ninth grade, Ross became an assistant pool manager. He pretty much ran the place. The next summer, after he turned sixteen, Ross would become a lifeguard, too. Consequently, the three friends spent virtually all their time together at the pool, working on their tan lines.

Ross's athleticism was already shaping his growing body; you could see the evidence in his broad shoulders, tapered torso, and strong, muscular legs. Sun and chlorine at the pool bleached his red hair to an appealing strawberry blond. He looked really good in the nylon racing suit he preferred to wear while he worked. Secretly, Alan admired the way Ross's ass looked in the suit.

Kenny was living up to his Scarecrow image—he seemed all arms and legs then, and his head looked a little small for his body. It would still be a few years before his Black Irish heritage filled out his body and covered it with soft, black hair. Around the pool he wore long surfer jams. Contrary to his hope, they only made his long, skinny legs look longer and skinnier.

Alan was a chubby child and a husky adolescent. He would end up a chunky adult once all his curves got sorted out. His body hair was already sprouting in some profusion. He was self-conscious about it but, in fact, because he was a dark blond, his hirsuteness wasn't very evident, although it did tend to highlight his curves in a flattering way. His favorite swimming suit was a spandex square-cut, which he thought made his ass look as good as Ross's. It didn't. However, it did make his package look the largest of the three, even though Kenny's was actually the largest.

The Fourth of July was a big party holiday in Goodland, the

only excuse for a civic get-together between Memorial Day and
Labor Day. Since everyone would be in his backyard or at the
park grilling hot dogs and hamburgers, the pool closed early.
Fireworks were at nine up at Renner Field, so the airport closed
early, too.

Ross was closing things down for the evening. Alan and
Kenny were the only other ones left, and they were already in
the men's locker room. They had already stripped off their suits
and were busily checking and comparing progress on their tan
lines when Ross finished clearing the women's locker room and
joined them.

They all got a small exhibitionistic frisson from being naked
in the locker room that, by design, had no roof but was open
to the sky; it was almost like being naked outside. Benches and
lockers occupied the middle of the room, behind the wall that
blocked visibility from the entrance. Toilets were at one end, the
showers at the other end behind another dividing wall. The floor
was smooth concrete except in the shower where it was a black-
and-white checkerboard of one-inch tiles.

With everyone else gone, there was plenty of hot water available for showers. Ross took his accustomed position at the middle showerhead; Alan was on his right and Kenny on his left,
their unvarying positions. At this age, custom and ritual were
important.

Also by custom, the usually talkative trio said little during
their showers. There seemed fewer topics for conversation when
they were naked together, although they did enjoy each other's
companionship.

Just a couple of weeks ago, a new ritual had suddenly
been established: Ross had asked Alan to wash his back. He'd
sounded casual enough about it, and though Alan thought it
was less casual than Ross made it sound, he certainly wasn't

going to question being given an excuse to run his hands across Ross's broad shoulders and down his tapered waist.

Today Ross made his request with just a glance and raised eyebrows in Alan's direction. Perhaps Ross thought the low-key approach kept Kenny from noticing. Kenny, of course, noticed but didn't much care one way or the other what Ross and Alan got up to, so long as he was part of the threesome.

Ross stood still and relaxed as Alan soaped his shoulders, then worked his way down along Ross's spine slowly and with more attention than needed. While most of Alan's concentration was devoted to Ross's back, he made certain that he didn't stand so close that his hard-on risked touching Ross's buttcheeks.

Soon, though, his soapy hands were caressing the firm curves of Ross's ass. Ross didn't stop him. Quite the contrary, in fact. When Alan's slippery hands moved down his asscrack, Ross spread his legs just a bit to draw Alan's hands further along. Alan's hand easily slipped under Ross, where he lightly fingered Ross's balls.

Ross may have moaned, but if he did the sound of the showers covered it up. He and Alan both enjoyed their separate sensations for what seemed like minutes before Ross broke the spell.

"Time for the long-jump event," Ross announced.

They all reacted with gusto. Each one grabbed his stiff dick and started beating off with individual technique that hadn't changed much in the last two years. What had changed is that each had begun to ejaculate with youthful vigor and volume.

Ross was always the speediest with his full-bore hand technique. He leaned his butt against the wall of the shower, yelled something incoherent, and shot one thick stream of cum that spattered across the tiles.

Alan was the silent one with his more sensual technique. Slow rhythmic strokes brought him to his climax after delicious anticipation. He, too, pressed his back against the shower wall as he shot his load.

Kenny had surprised and amazed the other two when he developed a method of clamping his fingers tightly around the head of his dick just as he reached his orgasm, jerking his hand down his dick and shooting off powerful spurts of cum with each stroke, managing several shots each time he beat off.

Ross was the first to count the number of tiles from the wall he had leaned against and the first splat of his semen on the floor. "A new personal best: twenty-seven inches!"

Alan counted next. "As usual, twenty-one inches."

Kenny counted last. His face showed a mixture of pride and embarrassment when he said, rather quietly, "Thirty-three inches."

Ross made no response. Alan smiled to himself with some satisfaction at Ross's comeuppance.

"That summer was an awakening for me," Alan told Donny. "Spending so much time at the pool with Ross and Kenny, I got to see lots of naked men with man-sized dicks, chlorine became my aphrodisiac of choice, and I developed a near fetish for locker rooms."

"I'm surprised I didn't run into you then," Donny said. "I spent quite a bit of time at the pool that summer, too. Probably for the same reasons."

"Were you as hairy then as you are now? I always noticed the hairy men, especially ones with mustaches."

"Not so much, I guess, although it was starting to grow in pretty thick by then. It made me very self-conscious in eleventh grade."

"Really? I always envied Ross so much when he started growing hair on his chest and then when his mustache started to come in. It made him so kissable."

"Did you ever?"

"What? Kiss him? No. I think he would have found it too queer."

"Really! So you two never had a relationship?"

"Not really. We were solid JO partners, but he never seemed to want to go beyond that."

Summer arrived early in Goodland the year the Friends of Dorothy were nearing the end of tenth grade. But then, Goodland was known for its extreme weather. When it was cold in Kansas, it was coldest in Goodland; when it was hot elsewhere, it was hottest in Goodland. Droughts lasted longer, snow drifted deeper, and tornadoes blew stronger. Residents took it as a challenge.

The threesome had come to feel that they were now too old for pajama parties or sleepovers, but camping out was a viable grown-up option. They used a small tent pitched in the generous backyard of Ross's house. There was no room behind the trailer where Alan lived with his mom. It would have been fun to camp out at the farm where Kenny lived, but his Uncle John didn't really approve of such adolescent frivolity.

Besides, Ross's mom always made treats for the events. The guys were a little old for cupcakes decorated with clown faces, but they were highly amused to the point of giggles when Mrs. O'Brien told Ross to take the tray of "goodies for his little friends" outside with them. The warm air was still and alive with the sound of crickets, and there was the occasional rumble from a distant thunderstorm, too far away to worry about.

Ross was stretched out on his sleeping bag in shorts and a T-shirt, hands behind his head, anticipating his new responsibilities as a lifeguard at the pool. Alan also looked forward to the summer at the pool and the chances it afforded him to look at naked men in general and Ross in particular. Kenny, tuckered out from a full school day and his chores at the farm, was already snoring softly.

"I think Kenny's asleep," Alan whispered.

"Sounds like," was Ross's ritual response.

Alan quietly repositioned himself so that he lay along Ross's side, his head at Ross's feet. He reached out and brushed his fingers lightly up and down Ross's leg; up and down, dancing delicately.

Each time Alan's fingers went up, they went further and further until they reached the bottom of Ross's shorts. Alan slipped his hand up underneath the shorts. He lightly fingered Ross's balls through his soft cotton Y-front briefs. Ross remained silent but his stiff dick strained against his underwear.

Alan pulled his hand out of Ross's shorts. He reached with both hands to the waistband and tugged. Ross lifted his hips so that Alan could pull the shorts and underwear down just enough to release Ross's dick. Ross then did the same to get at Alan's boner.

Jerking each other off was fun to do—and it was fun to have done, too—but there were shortcomings. Ross preferred that Alan use a firmer, rougher grip and pump more vigorously. Alan preferred a gentler, less frantic pace. Nevertheless, having someone else's hand around his hard-on, jerking off with unfamiliar and unpredictable sensations, brought each to climax quickly.

Alan held Ross's dick for a bit while his own erection subsided. Some of Ross's cum had pooled in the web of skin by the thumb of Alan's hand. He lifted it to his mouth and licked off the cum, tasting it for the first time. He was surprised by its saltiness. He was also surprised that it tasted good.

Ross seemed in a hurry to pull up his shorts; Alan liked leaving his down while his dick softened against his thigh, a small drop of cum stretching down his leg. Ross was often talkative after he and Alan jerked off, but tonight he seemed more thoughtful.

"We're going to have to stop doing this," he said at last.

After a pause Alan asked, "Why?"

"It's not right. My dad is already talking about sending me to law school so I can follow him in public service, and Mom is already talking about the type of woman I should marry for my career."

"That doesn't mean we have to stop fooling around."

"Yes it does. I can't be gay."

"Sure you can. Don't you like beating off together?"

"I mean I can't turn gay. I mustn't. I have to stop before it goes too far."

"What's that supposed to mean? It's not like it's cooties or something that can rub off."

"I know I can stop," Ross insisted, "before it's too late. It's a lifestyle and I can't do it if I'm going to go into politics. My dad talks about it all the time, how sick it is."

"Well, I think it's too late for me," Alan said.

"And what's that supposed to mean?"

"I've already gone too far, beat off too much, or whatever turns a person gay. It's not sick. I like doing it and I don't see a problem. I like going to the pool locker room and watching the naked men. I like to imagine what it would be like to hold a big, stiff dick in my hand, or maybe put one in my mouth. I imagine kissing a man some day, with tongue and everything, and I expect it will taste good. Gosh, I've probably turned gay already."

Ross was exasperated by Alan's sarcasm and this turn in the conversation. "Fine," he said, "whatever. Just don't try to kiss me."

"Fine. Whatever. Like I'd even want to."

Neither one said another word that night, but they listened

for quite some time to each other's heavy, angered and hurt breathing before falling asleep.

"That summer after tenth grade was okay," Alan told Donny. "We spent a lot of time at the pool as we always had, and we beat off a lot as we always had, but things started to feel different between us. Maybe we were just growing up."

Donny looked around for their waitress and indicated that he wanted more coffee when he caught her eye.

"Eleventh grade was definitely a bit of a strain," Alan continued.

"Because of the gay thing, you mean?"

"No. Not directly at least. It was more like we started noticing other things in the world around us. News, world events, other people—like you, for instance."

"Me!" Donny couldn't imagine. "Why me?"

"You were a senior and too busy to notice a mere junior, but when you first came to school with that rainbow flag on your backpack…"

"Oh yes! That would have been October. I did that for National Coming Out Day. I hoped someone would see it and feel less alone."

"I did! Up until then I'd thought I was the only homo in Goodland, maybe even in all of Kansas."

"I suspect I was also hoping that I'd meet at least one other gay person, too."

"Well, I was way too shy for that, but I thought you were the hottest looking guy in the whole school. I, um, thought a lot about kissing you."

"Mercy! You bring color to my cheeks, but I am honored. If only I'd known…"

"…What would you have done? You were a senior, I was an

invisible junior and we were worlds apart then. Anyway, I think Ross was a bit freaked out by the whole thing."

"By me? How? Why?"

"Apparently I mentioned your name more than just occasionally. One day toward spring we were having lunch and I was going on about something when Ross slammed his sandwich down on the table and shouted 'Donny this, Donny that—I am so sick of Donny! If Donny is so fucking perfect why don't you marry him!' "

"I was speechless, really, because I hadn't realized at all that I was doing it. Kenny said something like 'Jeez, Ross, lighten up.' Ross grabbed his stuff and stormed off. We never mentioned it again."

"Sounds like a little jealousy to me."

"Could be, but he wasn't the only one, let me tell you. I think Ross had a big crush on the basketball coach that fall."

"No kidding!"

"At least a serious case of hero worship. He was always going on about 'Coach this' and 'Coach that'—it was really kind of nauseating. Anyway, there was this time when I was meeting Ross after his practice, so I went to the school locker room looking for him. Most everyone had left and it was really quiet, although someone was still in the showers. I heard Ross's voice saying something and I was about to call out to him when I heard another voice talking to him."

"Ah. So he wasn't alone."

"The other voice was Coach's. He said something that made Ross laugh, but it made me feel a little dizzy. I don't even remember leaving the locker room, but I did somehow without being noticed."

"Wow. Do you think he and the coach…?"

"Oh no, I never saw any sign of that. I don't know how

innocent it was for Coach, but I'm pretty sure it was just a naive infatuation for Ross. Still…"

"It must have felt awful."

"It did. I don't think I ever trusted Ross again after that. But the one I really felt sorry for was Kenny."

"Really! Kenny? Why?"

"Kenny is such a sweet guy, never devious or manipulating or secretive. I think it confused him to be caught in the middle of all the drama between Ross and me. I suspect we hurt his feelings a lot, which we never intended to do."

"Did you get past those things with Ross?"

"Not really. I stopped talking about you as much—probably thought about you more, though. Ross seemed to get over his Coach crush after basketball season and then in the spring he started dating Melissa, which was a pretty obvious tactic."

"She was there today. I couldn't tell whether she looked more sad or relieved."

"Then, that summer before our senior year was the big blowup."

Ross and Alan and Kenny hadn't really spent much time together since the beginning of eleventh grade. At least not good, old-friends kind of time together. There'd been no treats for Ross's "little friends" for over a year, no non-sleepovers, no sperm long-jump events, no ritual lighting of the Sacred Flame. Their secret clubhouse by the grain elevators was overgrown and collapsing. Their lives were starting to head in different directions, but they hadn't yet noticed.

Some old habits persist until something happens to break them. As they had for more summers than they could remember, Alan and Kenny spent most of their time at the municipal pool. If you'd asked, they would have claimed there was nothing else to do for summers in the toe-jam of the universe.

It was the end of summer, the last week before the Labor Day Weekend, the last full week before the pool closed. So many people were away, visiting or vacationing before school started, that they very nearly had the pool to themselves. Alan and Kenny were there until closing and managed to exchange not a single word with Ross.

Alan and Kenny were the last ones to head into the locker room, and the last ones remaining while Ross was closing down the pool for the night. Neither seemed in a particular hurry—they weren't really on speaking terms with Ross, but they waited to leave when he did.

Both had stripped off their suits and were drying themselves in desultory fashion. Kenny's offhand manner caught Alan off guard when he asked, "Have you ever kissed a man before? I mean a real, romantic kiss?"

Alan hesitated, because he wanted to say yes. "Not yet, but I've thought about it a lot. I'd kiss Donny Doyle on the spot if he asked me, that's for sure."

"Don't you wonder what it's like? I mean open mouthed and with tongue and all?"

"Sure. You can practice kissing your pillow or your arm, but they sure don't have tongues."

Kenny giggled. "Do you want to try? You know, strictly for informational purposes."

"Sure, if you really want to."

Kenny took two steps to face Alan, and stood looking into Alan's eyes for a moment. They were standing close enough that their dicks, already hard, were touching.

They touched lips tentatively at first, then with more resolve. After settling the question of whose nose would go in which direction, they opened their mouths and their tongues touched at the tips. Alan had closed his eyes, but Kenny kept his eyes wide open.

After some seconds spent with Kenny's tongue exploring Alan's teeth, they pulled their mouths apart and stood in silent assessment.

Kenny asked first: "Did it work for you?"

"I think so. Some, at least. I'm sure I'd try it again."

Kenny nodded as though absorbing this datum. "What about that other thing? You know, having a guy's boner in your mouth. Is it good? Have you done that yet?"

"Not yet."

With no more warning than that, Kenny squatted in front of Alan and took Alan's erection fully into his mouth. Kenny rolled his tongue around Alan's dick and slid his lips along its length a time or two, but otherwise he wasn't really sure what to do.

They were so lost in the novelty of the sensations they were experiencing that neither heard Ross come into the locker room until he started shouting.

"Goddamn cocksucking homos!"

Frozen in place, they looked over at Ross, who stood in the doorway, his face red with rage.

"What the fuck are you doing now, you pervert! Trying to recruit Kenny? Get out! Get out! Both of you get out!"

Ross turned and left. Alan and Kenny snatched up their clothes, covered themselves enough to go outside, and left as quickly as they could without running. As they hurried away from the pool they could hear Ross slamming metal trash cans around and howling in rage, or pain, or both.

"Wow." Donny sipped from his mug of coffee—his third. "You know, I did hear something about something happening back then, but since I'd graduated already I didn't pay much attention. I didn't realize... That was pretty intense."

"At the time I was surprised by the vehemence of Ross's reaction."

Donny didn't really sound serious when he asked, "So, do you think the experience turned Kenny gay?"

"Nope. I think he just had a healthy curiosity. He's always been as straight as Ross wanted to be. I'm sure that Kenny is marrying Linda later this month because he's entirely content with his heterosexual lifestyle."

"You don't think Ross was actually straight, do you?"

"Probably not. Maybe. I don't know. He certainly wanted to be straight. At least when he was around me he did."

"But not when he was around me," Donny said, avoiding Alan's eyes when he said it.

"Oh?" Alan asked. "Is there something you know that I don't?"

"Well," Donny began, "you know that spot behind the junkyard—out by the grain elevators, on the other side of the tracks—where men go to cruise for sex?"

Alan affected an innocent air. "Do they?"

"As I'm sure you know, at least by hearsay. Anyway—and this all happened after you'd graduated and gone away to Emporia State—I went out there a few times, not like it was a frequent occurrence or anything..."

"Oh, of course not!"

"...And who should I run into but Ross O'Brien, who pretended not to recognize me. Now, I wouldn't want to speculate on his proclivities, but he seemed awfully intent on giving as many blow jobs to as many men as he could, and he desperately wanted me to fuck him, without a condom I might add. I refused."

"So," Alan said, "you have no doubt that Ross was gay."

"I have no doubt that Ross was one seriously conflicted dude, that's for sure."

Alan shook his head slowly. "Poor Ross. He got a lot of pressure at home to conform. His dad, the Big Sheriff, wanted him to grow up and be the important politician and live the straight lifestyle fantasy. I think he was always looking for his father's approval and never got it. His dad didn't even make it to our graduation."

Donny let a few moments of silence pass. "So, do you think Ross's death was an accident?"

Alan tried to look shocked but he wasn't really. "Are you suggesting that he drove his car into that tree on purpose?"

"You have to wonder. Full moonlit night, no ice on the road, no curve, no mechanical failures, no alcohol, no other cars, no obvious cause."

"I've wondered, I guess. Sometimes I feel guilty, like I could have been better to him that last year or two, or tried harder. We'd been such good friends. I don't know why it had to end the way it did. Could I have made some difference? Does it make any difference whether he died accidentally or not, now that he's gone? I don't know. I only know that it's all such a waste and so unnecessary."

Donny nodded. Again the silence stretched, but this time it was a shared, companionable silence. Donny reached his arm across the table and put his hand over Alan's.

"I'm sorry that I made you think about all this all over again," Donny said.

"Don't worry about it. It was good to remember. I need to remember."

"If you'll have coffee with me again, I promise to talk about happier, gayer subjects."

"I've got a better idea. Why don't you come with me to Kenny and Linda's wedding? I need a date."

"Really? You don't think they'd mind?"

"Kenny? No way. He's my best friend, after all. He'd be happy to see that I've finally met someone. I think he worries about me. So, what do you say? Is it a date?"

Donny didn't even have to think about it. "You bet it's a date."

THREE WEEKS TILL BEAR SEASON

C. B. Potts

Sometimes the absence of sound tells you more than its presence. Kenny frowned and stepped up onto a small rock outcropping alongside the trail, listening for the birds. He could hear none.

Contrary to popular rumor, an Adirondack morning is hardly quiet. That goes double in the fall, when chattering flocks of songbirds gorge on summer's last spoils, fattening themselves for the long flight south. Every last berry was worth fighting over, every captured gnat accompanied by a triumphant fanfare.

And yet now they were quiet. Only two things shut birds up: dark and danger. Dawn had just shed her gray silken shroud, revealing the first cerulean streaks of autumn brilliance wrapped across the sky, so it had to be the latter.

Kenny shifted his weight, listening.

There was a slight rustle in the grass. Not much, but in this silence, momentous. He'd passed by a big ol' mama bear and cub on his way out early this morning, rooting through a downed stump. Common sense dictated that he give the pair plenty of room—brown bears aren't at their best when they've got hibernation hanging heavy on their minds—but maybe he'd not gone far enough.

He gripped his deer rifle, grateful for the weight of it in his hand. It wouldn't do much against a riled-up brown bear, but it might buy him enough time to hightail his bony ass to safety.

Another rustle, closer. He scanned the woods, looking for blocky shadows. The birds that were about kept to their branches, which meant it was either too soon to fly or far, far too late.

Fuck. The trail ahead forked two ways. One would bring him out the back of Pytlak's orchard, where, more likely than not, he'd find whitetail grazing the apple trees. That'd been his original destination, and maybe he should stick to the plan. Widow Pytlak wouldn't be none too happy to see him—she preferred deer on the hoof to on the plate—but she'd let him in long enough to escape an angry bear.

The other way was way shorter, brought him flat down to one of the million nameless creeks that fed into Lake Champlain.

Snapping branches now, as whatever-it-was pushed through the nearby underbrush.

Kenny took to his heels. He couldn't outrun a brown bear, he figured, but he could sure the hell outswim one.

He launched himself, a startled pheasant in deep woods camo, and pushed down the narrow trail.

The crashing behind him grew louder. Closer. Nearing with every step, as he scrambled over snarled roots and awkward jutting slabs of skittering, splintering shale.

More snapping, crackling, breaking brush behind him.

Five more steps and the ground started getting softer. Slicker, slipperier, as ferns clustered at the side of the trail.

It was hard to keep his footing, but he was pretty motivated to stay upright and moving. The creek couldn't be far.

It wasn't. In fact, the sharp black ribbon of water had just come into sight when a beefy paw fell on his shoulder.

Kenny went sprawling, pushed off balance by his pursuer. All the wind was knocked out of him by the fall, kept out of him by the couple of hundred pounds that collapsed onto his back.

He tried to scramble away, but it wasn't happening. His captor was too big, too strong.

Kenny swallowed, preparing for the worst. He could feel the hot breath on the back of his neck, burning, wanting.

Teeth close to his ear.

And then:

"Kenny Collins, you sorry excuse for a bastard! How many times do I have to explain to you what dawn till dusk means?"

The weight on his back started to feel a whole lot better.

"Ranger LaCroix."

Maybe his legs splayed wider. Just a little. Maybe.

"I mean it, Kenny."

"Dawn's been and gone, Ranger."

"It wasn't when you set out. Sun hadn't even thought about coming up." Long fingers twined through Kenny's hair, pulling his face up out of the mud. "Let's not talk about them three doe you've already got hanging behind your garage. You're in a heap of trouble here, boy."

"What can I say?" Kenny brought his hips up, just high enough so his ass brushed against the unmistakable bulge trapped in Ranger LaCroix's uniform pants. "I'm a bad boy."

"Don't give me that bullshit." Kenny's face was suddenly in the mud again. "You can't be out here poaching deer."

"Screw you." Kenny spat the words out, pissed now. "Sun's up. T'aint nothing you can do about it, and you know it. So get off of my ass."

Those teeth were next to his ear again. "Oh, I will," Ranger
LaCroix hissed, pausing to take a small nip at Kenny's earlobe.
"But not until you've learned your lesson."

One hand reached under to Kenny's fly, working the stiff
leather awkwardly.

"What're you doing, Ranger?"

"Nothing, Kenny." Another bite, firmer this time, on the side
of the neck. "I'm as innocent as you are."

Ranger LaCroix's hand slid down the front of Kenny's jeans,
wrapped round his rapidly swelling cock. "And you feel pretty
damn innocent to me."

A slight squeeze, and Kenny was moaning.

"I swear, Ranger, I didn't do nothing...."

"Not for lack of trying, I reckon." A few awkward strokes
and then Kenny's jeans were being peeled down. "You need
something to keep you occupied. Make sure you stay out of
trouble."

Kenny shivered, his cock now hard and snaking up his stomach. "You volunteering for the job, Ranger?"

"Maybe." The air was cool against Kenny's ass, cooler between the cheeks being forced apart. Fingers slick with god-
knows-what pushed in. "If you think I'm man enough."

Kenny groaned, his hips rising to meet the thrusting fingers.
"Think you'll have to show me before I can answer you."

A zipper coming down can be remarkably loud in the wilderness.

"Smartass." The blunt head of Ranger LaCroix's cock pushed
against Kenny's pucker. "What d'you think so far?"

"Mmmm," Kenny replied, pushing back to envelop the probing cockhead. "So far, so good."

Ranger LaCroix dropped his ass onto his ankles, pivoting
Kenny upward in the process.

"Garrh!" Kenny cried, as the rest of the ranger's shaft was buried deep inside him. "Holy fuck!"

"Yeah," Ranger LaCroix agreed, wrapping one hand around Kenny's shaft. "You're so tight. So hot."

Then there was silence again—but this was the natural silence of the woods, punctuated by occasional feathered squabbles and the splashing of brook trout arcing ever so briefly toward heaven.

And, of course, all the rutting grunts and groans two sweaty men can manage. They added another layer of sound to the mix, a frenetic, earthy, needing symphony of lust, punctuated with *oh* and *yes* and *god* and other, less recognizable words.

Kenny was on his stomach again, hips cantilevered upward as Ranger LaCroix plowed into him. "Don't stop. I'll freakin' die if you do."

"T'aint planning on stopping," Ranger LaCroix groaned. "I'm just like you."

The ranger's hands were splayed in the mud beside Kenny's face, one thumb a few tantalizing inches from Kenny's mouth. He couldn't resist. With a smile, he started tonguing the short digit, tracing over the bumpy knuckle, the smooth expanse of fingernail, the calloused tip.

"Jesus, that's hot," Ranger LaCroix groaned, skewing a thrust so it bumped squarely against Kenny's prostate. "You've got a fuckin' awesome mouth. A pussy mouth. When I'm done riding your ass, I'm gonna get me a piece of that mouth of yours."

"Anytime," Kenny agreed, closing his lips around the ranger's thumb.

"Suck it, suck it, suck it," Ranger LaCroix urged, collapsing onto Kenny's back. "Oh, fucking holy god, I'm gonna come."

Kenny sucked harder, flexing his ass at the same time.

In response, the ranger bit his shoulder, bit it so hard it drew blood through the camo.

Sharp-edged pain ran alongside the sheer pleasure coursing through his system, too much for any man to bear. He came with a cry that sent the startled birds flying for their lives.

Ranger LaCroix chuckled, slowly rolling off of Kenny's back. "I take it that was good for you?"

Kenny sat up, eyed the ranger warily. "Let's just say you've got the job if you want it."

"Oh, I want it, all right." Ranger LaCroix's grin was broad and bright. It faded as he continued "But you keep this shit up, it might turn out to be my only job. Half the county's already talking about the mad poacher and his ranger boyfriend."

"Ah, screw them." Kenny grinned. "I can keep you in high style. You'll have venison year round."

"I mean it, Kenny." Ranger LaCroix reached for him, only now giving up a long, lingering kiss. "Can't you think of anything else to do in the wee hours of the morning besides go hunting?"

"A few ideas spring to mind," Kenny said, dipping down for another kiss. "They should hold me over. At least until bear season opens."

NOEL, FOR THE LAST TIME

Wayne Courtois

About a quarter mile from the house, down a narrow dirt road, the pond lay like a stain on the landscape. There wasn't much else to see on this part of the farm: a barren field, the partial shape of an abandoned barn, wheel-ruts leading to an old quarry that indented the woods. I stood on the pond's grassy bank and looked up at the diving platform, twenty feet above me. Noel's toes clenched the edge. I nearly held my breath, not wanting to move, till the platform finally creaked and he hit the water.

He surfaced, blowing water off his lips, curls leaking down his forehead. "Feels good," he said.

Those were the first words he'd spoken since we came down here, and they eased the tension a bit. I hadn't seen Noel in years, not since he'd left for New York. But when I was driving by the farmhouse and saw him sitting on the front porch, I had to stop. He'd miscalculated in choosing this weekend to surprise his family with a visit, since they were out of town. "Yeah, I know," he said. "Riley told me." He seemed almost shy, taking the hand I offered. Had we ever shook hands before? As my girlfriend's older brother, he was pretty much an unknown quantity. "He couldn't tell me where Matt was, though."

So it was up to me to tell him, and right away I saw why Riley, who was only the hired hand, hadn't dared; Noel blew up, yelling, stomping, sweeping photographs off the mantel: *Why the fuck didn't they tell me?*

I'd hoped that a swim in the pond might calm him down, but it was hard to tell. He stayed in one spot, treading water, either looking at nothing or looking inward. Then he raised an arm and let it fall, hard, striking the surface.

"Noel," I said.

He smacked the water again, harder.

"Noel!"

He looked at me, no favor in his dark, hooded eyes. All I could say was, "Take it easy."

His voice carried softly over the water: "Fuck you."

"He was seventeen. Dogs don't live forever."

I stripped down to my underwear, sat on the bank and stuck my feet in the water. They became cool, heavier than feet. As I eased down I scraped my back, but the pond took my body away from me, only to return it moments later, wanting air. I rose to feel the surface break over my face, and began to swim laps, recalling the first time Margaret had brought me here. It had been full dark then, with nothing but moonlight to see by.

"I'm not swimming," I'd said.

"What's going to hurt you?"

"Snapping turtles. Bloodsuckers. Snakes."

She always found it easy to laugh at me; I liked that. "We've got a saying where I come from," she'd said, tossing her hair back for the climb to the platform. "There's only one thing to do when you're scared of something."

"And what's that?"

She showed me. It was the first time I saw her dive, and I ached to see it again—the curl, the reach, a brushstroke ending in a splash. I waded in after her, and soon we were both pressed against the bank, tasting the pond on each other.

"Listen," she'd said. "Noel's here."

"That's Matt, hunting frogs."

"There's one frog that sounds too much like a frog to be a frog," she'd said.

Ri-bit. Noel swooped past us, in a dive that was almost a belly whopper. He never paid much attention to us, wasn't protective of his youngest sister. He was just a shadow passing a window as we necked in the dooryard, a creak overhead as we sank into the sofa—or footsteps moving up the gravel road, along with a deep, fading voice: "C'mere, Matt. Come on with me now." He kept the big Saint Bernard by his side, always.

Now Noel went under, came up sputtering, went under again. I gulped air and swam down, through layers of cold, colder, colder still, till my fingers brushed decay at the bottom. When I plunged my legs down, the muck formed a second skin from my toes to my knees. Flakes and shreds of old plant life roiled around, the merest brown against the dark water. I stayed until my lungs began to burn, then slowly rose, the muck shifting, dragging against my legs....

Something grabbed my shoulder.

Water burst into my throat. I doubled over to fight off choking. By the time I began to claw my way upward, Noel was high above me. Goddamn him! My lungs itched for air as the surface seemed to approach, then recede, over and over. Finally

I hauled myself up on the grass to lie choking and snorting.

In a few minutes I skimmed the water with my foot. Its touch connected with the moldy taste in my throat, and I knew I was through with swimming for the night. I looked over the landscape, which was still as a painting, not a bird or mosquito in motion. The edge of the sky held a leftover yellow, while the deepest blue jelled overhead. As I crossed the bank the grass rustled under my feet, a lonely sound.

Noel's clothes lay on the ground where he'd left them, with one addition: his briefs, soaked dark except for the white band. I called him. No answer. I looked up at the diving platform, walked to the foot of the ladder. "Noel!" No answer. I shook the ladder, its rungs so worn they looked like bones. "Damn it, I'm not coming up after you!"

I found my clothes and pulled them on, yanking my T-shirt into shape, lacing my sneakers too tight. I returned to the ladder again and said, "I'm going home." I meant it, yet I stayed where I was till I had to admit I couldn't leave without making sure he was all right.

No, I didn't like climbing, but anger got me started. By the time I was halfway up, my legs were shaking. Clenching my teeth against the urge to look down, I couldn't look straight ahead anymore, either: there was too much sky between the rungs. I closed my eyes and reached for another. Another. I squinted up to see the lip of the platform just above me, but the craving to look down was too much. I looked. The ground took a sickening twist.

"Grab my hand," Noel said.

I couldn't move, so he grabbed me, pulling me up by the arm. I sat down hard on the platform, which seemed to be turning slowly.

His voice came from above and behind me: "Thought you

were going home."

"Tell me," I said, trying to catch my breath. "Tell me why you had to get me up here."

"Did I get you up here? I didn't say a word. You got yourself up here."

"I was mad."

"Is that all?"

I looked at him then, standing there naked. He had the handsomeness that ran in the family, his eyes dark and hooded, like a bird of prey. His lean, strong build was familiar to me, but his dick wasn't—not hard like that, sticking out in front of him. I looked away, my face burning. I'd never seen a guy like that, not in the flesh, not that close.

"Go ahead and look," he said.

Just thinking of it made my legs start shaking, as if I were still on the ladder.

"I thought so," he said. He came closer, the platform creaking. When I looked up his head was coming down, his fingers tunneling warm through my hair. His tongue swelled in my mouth, tickling my palate, snagging cusps of teeth. I stretched my mouth to take more of him, my lips tingling against his stubble. He smelled of the pond, of himself. When he raised his head I rolled away, but his finger found the neck of my T-shirt. "I always thought so," he said, bending down again, using his mouth on the top of my spine as whole minutes grew and broke silently.

I followed him back to the house. He'd put his jeans back on but carried his T-shirt in his hand. I kept my eyes on his broad back, noticing how it tapered to his narrow waist. He led me up the lawn, across the porch, and through the front door—not my usual means of entry. The hallway, with its bare floor, coatrack, and faded brown wallpaper, was a face put on for the formal visitor. It seemed to be asking me, *What are you doing here?*

Beyond the hallway was the living room and its family of furniture—two worn sofas, a litter of chairs, a rocker, and a loveseat. It was a larger family than the one still living here, which had dwindled to three, Margaret and her parents. Noel and Jeannie, his other sister, were like so many who grew up in Maine: they craved places filled with people. Jeannie had only made it as far as Framingham, while Noel had struck off for New York. I was about to ask him for a cigarette—I'd left mine down by the pond—when he disappeared up the stairs. Was he expecting me to follow him? Instead I found a pack of his mother's cigarettes on the cluttered mantel behind the Franklin stove, and settled on the threadbare sofa I knew so well, my feet on the braided rug where Matt used to sleep. I wasn't about to leave this room, so loaded with familiarity, the kind you depended on when your closest neighbor lived over a mile away. In this case that would be Riley. It made me mad that Riley didn't tell Noel his dog had died, but I couldn't really blame him. He was, as people said in whispers, feebleminded. But why hadn't Noel's family written or called him to let him know his dog had died? Didn't anyone have the nerve? His mother would have; Pat had more nerve with him than anyone else. As the bitter tobacco of the unfiltered cigarette brushed my tongue I could almost hear her, scolding Noel as if he were the youngest, not the oldest: *Noel, where have you been? Who do you think you are? Noel, for the* last *time, don't drink from the milk pitcher! Take your shoes off when you come in from the barn, and wipe that smile off your face when I'm talking to you!*

Noel came downstairs with his arms full. He kicked some chairs aside, spread out a green and yellow quilt. "It's cooler down here," he said.

I stepped back, as far back as I could. Whatever had seemed possible down at the pond was impossible now. "Look, I have to go."

Not looking at me, he tried to pound shape into two flat pillows. "What's your hurry?"

I picked up one of the photos he'd knocked down earlier. A shot of Margaret, taken at the beach. It was one of very few pictures in the room with her face in it; usually she was the one behind the camera. I set it back on the mantel.

He came for a look. "Good old Maggie," he said.

That made me wince. "Don't call her that, she hates it."

"I'll call her what I want. She's my sister."

"Well..." It was time to say, "She's my girlfriend," but I was recalling how his mouth had felt on the back of my neck.

"Come here," he said. He was already close enough to touch.

I turned away, kicked at the braided rug. "I spent time with you tonight," I said, "because your dog died and I felt sorry for you. That's all."

He unzipped his jeans. I looked at him: there was no way I couldn't. When his jeans were around his ankles he reached down and adjusted himself. Probably his dick was sticky, he had to pry it free from his balls so it could grow. I had done that myself, countless times. But to see him do it...my legs started shaking again.

"Tell me you don't want me," he said. "Make me believe it, and I'll let you go."

I moved through the kitchen, letting the screen door bang behind me, but got no farther than the back steps, where I sat with my head in my hands. This had been one of Matt's favorite spots; he should have been within reach, whimpering as I scratched behind his ears. Instead the loneliness of a country night settled around me like pollen.

"Goodnight," Noel said, unexpectedly close, behind the screen door.

I couldn't answer, my voice would crack.

"Goodnight," he said again.

I wanted to say I was scared—scared of the feeling I'd had by the pond. Scared it would come back, scared it wouldn't. Scared of a future where I wouldn't be myself, but someone else.

"We're safe," he said. "No one'll bother us."

I turned to face him, rough-edged against the screen. "I'm scared," I said.

He spoke so softly I could barely hear him: "There's only one thing to do when you're scared of something."

"Lights on or off?"

"I want to see you," I said.

The living room light was still burning. Reaching down, I felt where he had fucked me. Pain flexed around my fingers, but they came up without blood. No real damage; the pain would go away. But the more I tried to ignore it, the more it kept me awake. Noel slept with his back toward me, didn't stir as I swung my legs from the quilt and found my watch in my jeans pocket. I was surprised to see it was only eleven o'clock. I was more surprised to find my hip pocket empty; my wallet was gone. I could almost see it where it must have fallen, on the grass by the pond.

Restless, I turned off the light and stepped into the kitchen. Cigarettes and matches lay in moonlight on the windowsill. No headlights passed on the county road as I smoked in the dark, recalling times when I'd sat here watching for Margaret's yellow VW to come shouldering over the hill. The car, an old Beetle, had once belonged to Noel. He sold it to her for more than it was worth. For a long time she kept everything he'd left in it, from old crushed sneakers and sweaty T-shirts to the Marlboro butts in the ashtray. "Smells like my brother in here," she'd say, opening the car in stuffy weather. And what would she say if she were here now? "Gil, *you* smell like my brother." It was true. Each time I raised the cigarette to my lips I caught his scent on my fingers—the scent of another man, so new, so fertile and deep, like the smell of the pond.

The house creaked, settling into itself. I rested my head on my arms and began to drift. Once I thought I heard Matt's nails on the linoleum, but it was only the clock near the stove, out of sight from where I sat. Counting seconds, I fell asleep.

The metallic hum of the refrigerator woke me. Enough time had passed for my neck to grow stiff, but that was nothing compared to the hunger I felt. Lover's appetite, Margaret would say. My bare feet made ripping sounds on the linoleum as I crossed to the counter where the cake plate sat. Lifting its cover released a whiff of chocolate. I sank my fingers into the cake—a Bundt cake with a fudge middle—and tore a hunk free and ate. Soon a thick sweetness coated the spot where my hunger had been. Licking my fingers, I suddenly craved milk. I opened the refrigerator gently and lifted the pitcher to my lips, violating a family rule. The flat-tasting raw milk loosened nuggets of chocolate from between my teeth, their flavor licking the back of my throat like a passion I'd stored up for years without knowing it. I closed my eyes and there we were, Noel and me, rising, falling, flowing into each other on the green and yellow quilt.

After fucking me, he'd flipped me over. My dick stood achingly hard between us. I wanted him to touch it, but as seconds passed and he didn't move, just hovered above me, I grabbed it myself. His eyes flickered: this was what he wanted. "Bring yourself off," he said, his voice husky. With him watching, my dick felt ten times bigger, still growing even as it leaped through my fist. When I came I shouted with each spurt. We were both soaked, the air filled with the smells of sweat and hot cum. I grabbed his upper arms and pulled him down. Before I knew it I was sucking my cum from his chest hair. Reaching down to feel him hard again. Pulling at him with my fist while my other hand cupped his balls, heavy yet fragile, like raised dough. I jacked him off, loving the way his dickhead slid through my fingers, knowing how it must feel. He shot all over my face, his hot cum sliding down my forehead and cheeks. We were soaked again—sticky, too, our chests plastered together as we kissed. When he finally rolled off me his skin tore at mine, stinging like sunburn. Not touching, heads turned toward each other, we finally drifted, our lips moving soundlessly in the moonlight, as if to repeat what our bodies had already said.

As I returned to the living room the farmhouse creaked and snapped like an old tree in a windstorm—nothing unusual for a two-hundred-year-old house. Noel sat up, everything clear in the moonlight except his expression as he said, "Thought maybe you'd left." Before I could say anything he lay back down, and was snoring by the time I was next to him again, wondering. Was that how it usually went—they'd leave in the middle of the night, without saying good-bye? I moved closer to him. Closer still. Each time he grunted, moved away.

I woke to a room where sunlight took familiar shapes: a chair, a sofa, the gleaming floor beyond my toes. My body was stiff as I sat up, tasting stale cigarettes, milk, chocolate. Noel stood naked in the doorway. The fact of him there, facing me the way a naked straight man never would, unsettled the world again.

"It's late," he said.

"What time is it?"

"Almost nine."

"That's late? On a Sunday morning?"

"Milking's been done already."

Milking. That meant Riley. "Did he see anything?"

"Who cares? Nothing happened here that he hasn't seen before."

I rolled the implications of that around in my cheek. Already this day was too much, too soon. It didn't help when Noel kicked something that spun, clattered, and rang to a stop near my feet.

"What's this?" he asked.

It was a large aluminum mixing bowl, with some powdery crumbs of dog chow at the bottom. "You know what it is," I said.

He sat on the sofa and leaned toward me, his hands on his knees. "Where is he?"

I hugged a pillow against my chest, just to put something more between us. "You're crazy."

"Don't say that." He drove his fist into a cushion. "I don't like it."

"You won't like this, either, but the dog is dead. Can we get that settled?"

"Then why was his bowl still in the barn? Why is there fifty pounds of dog chow under the sink?"

"Because the rest of the family is just like you—they can't let go."

His shoulders sagged. "Tell me where they buried him."

"I wasn't here when they buried him."

"You're lying."

"Sure. I can't call you crazy, but you can call me a liar." I'd twisted myself up in the quilt till it was too confining. Breaking free would leave me naked in front of him, so I kicked only part of it loose, so I could stretch my legs. "I lost my wallet. I'll have to go back to the pond to look for it."

He got to his feet, came close enough to pick up the bowl. "I'll be in the kitchen."

My clothes had a crumpled, desperate look, as if they'd spent the night trying to escape from the floor. As I picked up my jeans I moved my head to shoo a fly from my arm, and again caught Noel's scent on my skin. I sniffed my arms, my hands; I sat on the quilt to bring my nose to my thighs. I touched his pillow, smelling of hair, sleep, troubled breath. The quilt slid along the floor as I gathered up its folds, pressing my face into them. When I looked up, I saw how dirty the windows were, how the room would be even brighter if they were clean. Yet I liked the way their veils of dirt obscured the view. There could be anything out there—new ways of being, of feeling, all the same under the sun.

In the kitchen I poured a steaming mug of coffee and carried it to the table, where Noel sat picking his lip with an unlit cigarette. Suddenly he looked at me and asked, "How old are you?"

"Twenty-four."

"People say you've got your whole life ahead of you? Ever hear that one?" He got up, rinsed his coffee mug in the sink. "Got a lot ahead of me, too. Fading away, or burning out? I think it's burning out, that's what my story is. Don't belong in the city. Don't belong here, either. Never did." He grabbed a dishtowel and swabbed around the cake plate. "All these crumbs. You do this?"

"I got hungry during the night."

"Lover's appetite... What's wrong?"

I wiped the frown off my face. "Nothing. Sometimes you use expressions she uses."

"Well, that's what you get for sleeping around in the same

family." He got a knife, sliced the cake to a clean edge and scraped the crumbs into the trash. "They ever talk about me?"

"Sure," I lied. Not even Margaret mentioned Noel much anymore. She'd cleaned him out of her car long ago.

He leaned against the counter, sucked chocolate from his thumb. "They know about me. I know they do."

I thought about that. "I'm not so sure."

"'Course they know. A guy my age who never had a girl?"

With a shock I realized that, though he might still look and act a lot like a high school kid, Noel must be in his early thirties. I stared out the window in the direction of Portland, where I'd always lived, and thought about the men who grew up in the country and stayed there—men who, by the time they were Noel's age, had fat wives and several kids. Poker nights and Sunday services. Backbreaking work from early in the day, cussing under the sun. Yes, Noel had turned out differently, as few did. Hardly anyone, in fact. "As far as anyone knows, you're just a loner," I said.

"Oh, they know. It just never gets mentioned. That way it's not real. It's knowing and not knowing at the same time."

I shrugged. "What difference does it make? You don't live here anymore."

For a half second he looked as if he might deny that. Then his eyes went hard. "You knew about me. That's why you stopped here last night."

"Look, I drove by, saw you sitting out there, and thought I'd stop. I didn't know what would happen."

"Bullshit." His hands made fists, then relaxed. He finally lit the cigarette that had been hanging from his mouth. "Well, fuck. Who cares. It was just another one-night stand."

"No." Anger pulled me to my feet. "Not just another one-night stand. For me there's only been Margaret. I've never slept with another woman, and I sure as hell never slept with a guy before."

He blew a smoke ring. "Well, I won't tell Margaret I tricked with her boyfriend, if that's what you're worried about."

"I didn't say I was worried about anything." I went over to him where he leaned against the counter. The line of his mouth was hard, but something in his eyes said, *Yes, I remember.* I brought my lips close. He didn't resist when I fitted my mouth over his. Our tongues slid against each other. At the same moment we grabbed at each other's jeans, unbuttoning, unzipping them. No underwear today. I hefted his cock, already half hard, and dropped to my knees. Took his dickhead in my mouth, surprised at its heat. He ground his hips in pleasure. I took another inch of him in, licking the underside, wondering how I could possibly take more. But it happened all by itself, his dickhead at the back of my throat, its smoothness, like the skin of a ripe fruit, belying its strength. His hips continued to move as he fucked my mouth. I reached to grab his asscheeks. His ass was hairy, curls tickling my fingers. His thrusts grew stronger. He gripped the back of my head, using me, filling me with his soft explosion, his bittersweet taste. I swallowed because I didn't know what else to do; I swallowed because I wanted to.

His cock was still mostly hard when he pulled it from my mouth. "You've never had this, either, have you?" he said. "Let's trade places."

My body, with a new mind of its own, wouldn't do what I wanted. I was all swollen, aching parts. "I can't stand up," I said, laughing at my own helplessness. Propping my shoulders against the refrigerator was the best I could do.

"Doesn't matter." He stepped free of the jeans bunched around his ankles and dropped to his knees, lowered himself between my legs. As his mouth approached my cock I felt it might tear itself free to meet him halfway. Nothing could stop the shaking, the fluttering of muscles throughout my body, just as nothing would ever make me forget the sight of his mouth taking me in, the hollows in his cheeks as he sucked. The reverse of what I'd felt a minute ago, the plum of my dickhead against his palate now, his tongue on the underside, just rough enough to make me crazy. My toes curled, my fingernails scraped at the linoleum. "Oh Jesus, that's good," I said, growling like a dog. I wanted two of him: two tongues, one filling my mouth, the other working my dickhead.

I thought my hips would leave their sockets, I fucked his mouth so hard. Filled him with cum, spraying down his throat. He swallowed, just as I had, and wiped his mouth with the back of his hand as he stood, leaving me too soon, my dick still half erect, ass plastered to the floor.

"Let's go," he said, pulling on his jeans.

I'd forgotten that we had anywhere to go, anything else to do.

He kept ahead of me all the way to the pond. It looked different in the daytime—yellowish green with pollen, pockets of yellow scum in the corners. I saw my cigarettes and matches, which had been soaked with dew and sunburned dry; but my wallet wasn't where I thought it would be. I kicked through the grass, swearing under my breath. Losing my wallet meant losing things I might not miss, till each tiny absence came around like a time bomb. I was out thirty bucks for sure, plus two credit cards and my license. Getting home without money might be a problem: I wasn't sure I had enough gas. So I retraced my steps, the sun like hands pressing on the back of my neck.

When I met up with Noel I said, "I can't find the fucking thing."

"So what are you going to do?"

"Before I do anything else I'm going to take a swim." I walked to the other end of the pond and stripped, keeping my back to him, and slid into the water. Its clinging warmth shocked me, and I climbed out in worse shape than before, scraping a slimy feel from my face. The water smelled like piss, and though pollen didn't usually bother me I had a sneezing fit that left my nose stinging.

Noel was sitting on the bank, his T-shirt on the grass beside him. "You'll catch hell for going home without your wallet."

"I'm not a fucking kid, Noel. Besides, I live by myself." I sat and used a handful of grass to scrub scum from my foot. I heard him moving, felt his hand on my shoulder.

"I need to know something," he said.

I looked up at him. "Me too. Do they always leave in the middle of the night?"

He looked around, carefully, as if anything around us could have changed. "I need to know where Matt's buried."

Shaking off his hand, I got up to pull on my jeans and T-shirt. "They'll tell you when they get home."

"No, they won't. I'm taking the next bus out. They won't even know I was here."

"Riley will tell them."

"Not when I get through with him, he won't."

"What makes you think I won't tell them?"

"You've got a secret to keep."

True enough. What I didn't know was the size of the secret. Was sleeping with him the extent of it, or was it something larger, closer to the matter of who I was? I finished lacing up my sneakers, tying them so tightly my feet ached. "I ought to be getting home."

"Why? There's nobody expecting you."

"Well, there was nobody expecting me here, either."

He snorted. "I always expected you, sooner or later."

"Oh, fuck you."

It felt good to strike out on the gravel road, away from him—till I remembered I needed a favor. Shit. I turned and said, "I'm not sure I've got enough gas to get home. If I can borrow a couple of bucks from you, I'll make sure you get it back."

I half expected him to refuse, but he pulled a wallet from his pocket—my wallet. Seeing it in his hand, I realized I'd known all along that he had it; I was ignoring the obvious, or trying to. He threw the wallet to land in the road between us, with Margaret's photo face up in a plastic window. It was her high school graduation picture, which didn't look much like her anymore. Now she had tight curls where her long hair used to be; and she had plans—the two of us getting married, her own photography studio bringing in money while I wrote novels. If anyone had told me that I could laugh, laugh hopelessly while thinking of this... I looked at Noel, who had so suddenly become the one person on earth who knew me. I saw how it could be, loving a man—how it wasn't just about bodies, what flesh alone could feel. And I saw how it would make my life impossible. Before I could stop myself I blurted, "There's nobody else here."

He shrugged. "Sure there is."

That sour laugh again: I couldn't help it. "Don't tell me to go to Riley."

"You won't have to. You'll see."

"Is that it? I'll *see*?"

Another shrug. "That's all anybody gets."

I looked at him, standing there with his thumbs hooked in his belt loops—did city boys do that? Needing him was like a bubble about to break, I didn't know if I could stand it. I walked up to him, not caring what he did as long as he was still there, because nothing had changed in that hot minute under the sun.

"I want you to fuck me," I told him. "Right here."

He started to back off. "The hell—"

"That's right." I grabbed the waist of his jeans, unbuttoned them with one tug. I wanted him to know I'd always been expecting him, too, even if it was fresh news to me. But Noel had been with me for a long time. Those dark hairs leading down from his navel to his groin—I knew them as well as I knew my own.

He stretched out on the grass. I got on top. The noon sun was stinging. His dick was hard as ever as I guided it in. I was so hungry I didn't care if it hurt, and that helped it not to. Then he began to grind upward, into me, and I gladly gave up control. Gave up my silence, too, the wordlessness of the night before. "Fuck me like you never fucked anybody," I said. "Make it the fuck of my life."

We ended up yards from where we'd started, having rolled over several times. I wanted his dick to stay inside me, felt the loss when he slid free. I'd fired another cumload on his chest, which he'd rubbed into his skin absentmindedly. We found our clothes—he nearly put my jeans on instead of his.

"Look," he said, spotting something over my shoulder.

In the country, animals have a way of just showing up. So I wasn't surprised when I turned to see a black mutt come tearing lickety-split down the gravel road. He started skidding to a stop yards away from me, bumped my legs just the same, then leaped to plant dusty paws on my belly and look up in yellow-eyed wonder as I scratched his head. Then he took off for Noel, who squatted to let the dog lick his face.

"Dog stinks," he said. "He's rolled in every kind of shit there is."

He was right, my hands were pungent. "Whose dog is it?"

"How the hell should I know?"

The dog came at me again, raising dust around my ankles. I lit a cigarette that had spent the night outdoors. It had an odd, fragile taste. When I looked at Noel again he seemed different. He looked about as sturdy as the broken barn far behind him, his mouth wanting to move in all directions at once. Would he look any less lonely surrounded by a city? I asked him, "You didn't really come up here just for the weekend, did you?"

He kicked up dirt. "Maybe I didn't know what I was doing. Doesn't matter now. I'm taking the next bus back."

"So you kept your place in New York?"

"Sort of."

"Well, as long as you're leaving, why don't you come with me? I'll give you a ride to the bus station."

The dog ran ahead, which seemed to make the road longer as we walked, like the silence between us. Lost in our separate thoughts, neither of us even noticed the dog tearing back toward us, a sudden blur and bump against Noel's legs, nearly knocking him down. It was canine exuberance all over again, the dog leaping at Noel as he twisted away, his hands covering his face as if the dust had landed in his eyes. Then he was on his knees, gathering the dog into a wriggling black armful. His shoulders rose and fell, just once. And I knew it wasn't just Noel I was seeing: it was Noel for the last time. He wouldn't be coming back this way again.

The dog broke free, was dancing around me as I put my hands on Noel's shoulders. "Hey."

He looked up, squinting.

"Come on," I said.

I led him back down the road. Almost halfway to the pond I stopped, poked through some bushes, moved a bit farther and poked again, revealing a thin gray path.

"It's over there," I said. "Margaret marked it with a stone."

He followed. The black dog ran ahead.

DRUM STONE

Dominic Santi

I felt the drums beating in my bones. The steady rhythm throbbed through me like a blood pulse as I breathed in the clouds of thick, sweet haze in the summer darkness. Not that I'd smoked much tonight, just enough for my part of the ceremony. But I'd been away from the rez for over ten years—too long to be gone off to the city, no matter how good my job was. And too long, I was discovering, to be away from what my grandfather had always called "the good tobacco."

Much as I didn't want to admit it, I was stoned. As soon as I could politely excuse myself, I slipped away from the fire and went back to my tent to sleep it off. With my head still floating, I lay back on my sleeping bag and tried not to move much. I was hoping for a breeze, something to take the edge off the heat and humidity. Instead, all I felt were the vibrations of the drums, coming through the ground as much as through my ears.

After a while, I had to laugh. In spite of my wooziness, the drums always made me hard. Tonight was no exception. When

I finally got uncomfortable enough, I reached down and unbuttoned my jeans, pulling my warm flesh out through the open *V* and into my hand. I pressed my shoulders back into the down-filled bag, settling in to get comfortable. Skin on skin felt good. My cock and balls were heavy as they stretched out to breathe in the thick night air.

I smiled as I stroked upward, drawing the heated blood further into my hand. A new singer was starting—Dave Two-Elks. Nobody else has a voice as clear as his. Thinking of Dave always turned me on. I shivered, feeling the heat in my hand as my cock became fully engorged. Dave and I had gone to high school together, even been on the same drum for a while, years ago. Dave was one gorgeous man. He looked like a warrior from the old days—tall and strong and proud. His long, straight black hair reached almost to his waist. His coppery skin was even darker than mine, his eyes so dark they were almost black on black. What that man looked like in buckskin should have been illegal.

Dave was straight as an arrow. He'd never minded that I wasn't. He'd even set me up on a couple of blind dates with guys he'd met on the powwow circuit after I moved to Minneapolis. He respected the tradition of two-spirit people. But he'd made it plain his interest was in chicks. If he'd ever figured out how I felt about him, he never let on. We'd stayed good friends.

Dave was the one who'd introduced me to Snow Fox, all those years ago. I shuddered as I stroked my cock all the way to the tip, remembering. Snow Fox had been one cool old man. Queer as they come, and with a knowledge of the old ways and traditions that always left me awestruck. When I met him, I'd been sullen and withdrawn—nineteen years old and bitter as a man could be over what I felt was the curse of being born gay and *Nishanabi* in the hetero white man's world. I'd started drinking, which meant I'd had to leave the traditional drum I'd been on.

Snow Fox was the one who'd led me back to myself. He'd had strong medicine. Even now, I grinned as I remembered the first day he'd dragged my surly young butt out into the forest. He'd taught me the ways of loving another man until my cock stood up straight and hard as a pine tree dripping sap. I'd come so many times I'd thought my balls were empty. Then he'd bent me over a stump and fucked my cherry hole until I howled. I'd looked down, stunned, between where my hands were braced on that stump, and watched my wildly waving cock spurting my juices out onto the blanket of leaves beneath my bare feet. My thick cum had splattered hot and heavy into the cool autumn air, the last strand drooling down like a thread of spider web connecting me to the damp yellow birch leaves. I'd still been shaking when Snow Fox grabbed my waist and yanked me back hard against him. I grunted as he pulled me up onto my toes and stretched my asshole even wider over his long, thick pole. The old man told me later my clenching ass muscles had pushed him right over the edge.

He'd held me like that for a long time, letting me feel the strength of his arms holding me, and the hard, flat planes of his belly pressing against my back while he surged into me. Then, as he relaxed, he'd slapped my ass and started laughing. Deep, rolling belly laughs that vibrated right up inside me. And finally, I'd laughed, too, pretty sheepishly actually, trying to swallow with my sore throat as I'd realized his cum-slicked cock was still buried deep in my ass and it felt *good*. He'd told me before I wasn't cursed, but now I believed!

I'd like to say my life had been great after that little revelation, and that I hadn't had a drop to drink since then, but that's not true. I did stop drinking more than an occasional beer with

my friends, though that was still too much to go back on the
drum. But by then I was getting more assimilated anyway. I just
didn't seem to fit in on the rez anymore. So, when I got the
job offer in the Twin Cities, I didn't think twice about accept-
ing. I said good-bye to my friends on a Friday, spent that night
with Snow Fox sucking and fucking and letting him do things to
my asshole I never dreamed a human being could do. Saturday
morning I cut my hair, got on the bus, and I was gone.

I remember looking out the dirty windows of the Greyhound
as we passed the touristy trading post mini-mall. I felt like a visitor leaving. All I could think about was my new job and my new
life. I fell asleep as we pulled onto the highway, the trees blurring
into a green haze.

But as I dreamed of my new world, my hand was still wrapped
around the amulet Snow Fox had given me the night before. It
was an old river stone, an agate, about three inches by one inch,
worn completely smooth with age and touching. Snow Fox said
it was ancient, passed down from one man to the next. He said
it was powerful medicine. All I knew was that when he'd fucked
that stone deep up my asshole, singing while he slid it back and
forth through his puddled cum, I came so hard I thought my
bones would break. I'd shouted to the stars, sucking the amulet
so far up my ass he'd had to pull it back out by the leather thong
that was threaded through the eye of the stone. And when he'd
pulled it out... I shuddered even now just thinking about it. It felt
so good I hadn't been able to draw in enough air to breathe.

Over the years, that little stone had turned out to be really
lucky. I always wore it under my shirt, against my skin. It had
the best gaydar in the world: the stone would feel like it was
starting to hum and quiver, heating just the slightest bit against
my skin. Even in three-piece-suit boardrooms, I'd look up to
find someone looking at me with the kind of lingering eye

contact that meant that man and I were going to spend time naked together.

Sometimes, when I was beating off, I'd slip the leather thong over my head and let the stone slide down my belly. I'd stroke the stone over my cock like I was painting the veins until they stood out blue against my skin, then cuddle the stone beneath the folded edges of my foreskin. It felt like the stone buzzed with electrical current when precum touched it. Sometimes, I laid the stone on my balls, wrapped the thong around my sac, and jerked off hard and fast, just so I could hear myself howl.

And sometimes, especially when I was lonely or confused, I tucked the stone up my ass for company. I know that sounds weird, but it was easier to think that way. And the stone didn't distract me. It made me so horny I always had to jerk off first anyway. If I used any lube other than warm, fresh semen, that rock felt like sandpaper. But covered with cum, it slid right up my asshole and made itself at home. All I had to do was hum, and my thoughts would clear, especially if I was chanting one of the old songs. I figured out a lot of business deals that way, all relaxed, sitting there naked at my computer, humming or singing softly to myself, with the thong wrapped around me like a cock ring so the stone wouldn't slide too far up and get lost. The thong was leather, so I had to replace it every couple of months. But that was a small price to pay for contentment.

Dave Two-Elks had invited me back for this year's homecoming and powwow. I hadn't been on the rez in almost eight years, since Snow Fox died. But tonight, being here felt like old times again, listening to the drums with my friends while we smoked and talked and ate fry bread and venison steaks. Maybe it was the way I was at peace with myself now. But for the first time, being back felt like a homecoming.

I'd even felt the stone humming tonight. But by then, I was

feeling the effects of the good tobacco big-time. When I'd stumbled back to my tent, I'd closed the screen to keep out the mosquitoes but kept the flap open so I could see the stars. By the time Dave's drum really got going, my head was actually starting to clear. I was feeling just a nice, mellow haze as I lay there, stroking my cock to the drumbeat while I looked up at the sky. The stone still felt like it was humming against my chest. I reached up to I slide it over my head so I could rub it against my cock.

I had the thong wrapped around my wrist and my dick in my hand when a shadow fell over the doorway. Somebody was hunching down toward me. His silhouette had a relaxed stance, although his movements were cautious.

"Hey, man, you in there?"

The shadow scratched on the tent flap as he spoke. I recognized the voice from earlier in the evening—Greg Dupont. We'd gone to high school together, too. Dave had introduced us again tonight when we hadn't recognized each other. Greg had left the rez even before I had, going into the navy, though I'd heard he had come back a couple years ago and was now working as an electrician for the tribe. I liked his voice. He laughed a lot.

"Yeah, I'm here," I said, trying not to laugh at myself as I sat up and slipped the leather thong back over my head. Even though I'd tugged my shirt down over my jeans, I was still too hard to button my pants—and just buzzed enough to not really care that I wasn't quite dressed for company. I opened the screen and motioned him in, zipping the screen back up fast before the bugs got in.

"Guess I'm a little loopy from not smoking for a while."

"It does that to you," Greg laughed. "I saw you leave the fire. Thought I'd come by and see how you were doing—maybe catch up on old times."

As he spoke, Greg squatted down on the floor next to me, just inside the door. I could see the outline of his long, thick hair against the starlight. Maybe my other senses were more sensitive in the darkness, but I was suddenly very aware that his hair and clothes smelled like wood smoke and the good, healthy sweat he'd worked up dancing. I like the scent of fresh sweat on a man. The ground was vibrating with the power of the drumbeats and Dave's singing. Suddenly all I could think was how much I wanted to touch Greg's hair.

"Long time," I said softly, wiping my palms on my thighs. I clenched my hands against the denim to keep from reaching toward him.

"Too long."

Whatever else Greg said was lost in the throbbing of the drums, but it didn't matter. If anything, his voice had been thicker than mine. My head finally cleared enough for me to recognize what the stone was telling me.

As Dave's song raised shivers on my arms, I leaned forward, sinking my hands into soft, silky handfuls of Greg's hair. I pulled him close, kissing him full on the mouth.

Greg's lips were soft and wet, parting as I probed them. I jumped at the fire of our tongues touching. Between us, the stone was almost buzzing. Without thinking, I ripped my shirt open, reached out and yanked his flannel off. Then our chests were touching, smooth skin to hard muscle, our nipples shivering as the stone pulsed over our hearts.

"What is that, man?" Greg's voice sounded almost reverent, his hair falling forward as he looked down between us.

The drums were so loud I felt his breath more than heard him, but I was still stunned. No one else but Snow Fox had ever said he felt the stone with me. But I couldn't think of the words to explain it. I nuzzled into the soft rhythm of Greg's breath, licking up the pulse line of his throat as the drums and the stone throbbed against our skin.

My open shirt had revealed my raging hard-on, now pressed against the front of Greg's jeans. Panting, he broke away. Without saying another word, he leaned down and took my cock into his mouth—and all the way down his throat. I gasped like I couldn't get enough air into my lungs. This man was no stranger to cocksucking. And he was humming, his throat a warm, wet blanket of vibration wrapped all the way down my shaft.

I lasted about two seconds. I pulled back as I started to spurt, but Greg wrapped his arms around me. He kept me in his mouth with strong arms that I couldn't pull away from, as my cock spilled onto his tongue. Then I realized he wasn't swallowing. He was holding my cum in his mouth, tasting it, smiling at me.

Suddenly I knew what else the stone was telling me to do.

"Don't swallow it, man," I whispered. "At least not yet."

He raised his eyebrows, but nodded, his soft spermy lips glistening in the rising moonlight.

I sat back on my haunches, tearing off the rest of my clothes in a frenzy, then his. I carefully lifted the leather thong over my head and, holding the stone in my fingers, I put it into his mouth.

His eyes opened wide in shock as the buzz touched his tongue. I drew the stone out, a silvery trail of cum and saliva following it from his lips.

"Use the rest for lube and fuck me."

I rolled back onto my sleeping bag, lifting my hips and pulling my knees high and back. Greg leaned forward and, for just a second, I felt the heat of his tongue on my anus, pushing my cum and his spit against and into me. Then my breath caught as his hot, thick cock glided into me, stretching me wider and wider as he sank in to the hilt on his first stroke.

"Oh, fuck, man! Fuck, you feel good!" he gasped. His arms shook as he braced himself over me.

But instead of pounding into me, Greg leaned forward and kissed me, swallowing me long and deep as our juices mingled on our tongues. His naked skin was hot as our smooth, sweaty bodies pressed together. My blood pulsed with the drum song. I wanted his blood to sing, too. As his tongue snaked down my throat again, I leaned over and pressed the slick, cum-covered stone past the hot gate of his sphincter and deep up inside him.

His cry tore the night air, but the sound was lost in the shrill of Dave's singing and the screaming ululations of the drum-driven crowd. Greg rose up on his arms, pumping into me with long, hard strokes—tip to hilt each time. I felt the drums in each stroke, the thrum and cry of Dave's voice and the ancient song vibrating directly on my joyspot. Greg was inside of me. Dave was inside of me. The drums were inside of me.

Dave's song ended on a long cry that filled the camp. Our voices joined his in a howl of pure ecstasy as Greg's body surged into mine and my balls exploded again. Greg's cock spurted against my prostate, pressing the cum out of me to land hot and musky on our smooth, sweaty skin. With a groan, Greg collapsed, his arms wrapped tight around me. He laughed softly, his chest and belly sliding on the sticky puddle that glued us together.

We lay that way for a long time, our breathing slowly floating back to normal. When I finally heard Greg's voice again, he was speaking softly. I didn't understand enough of our language to catch all that he said, and his face was buried deep in my neck. But I knew they weren't just words of passion. He lifted his head, shaking his hair back over his shoulders. As the fire flared outside, I saw the smile lighting his face. Then he bent back down, letting his hair fall softly onto my face and neck as he very slowly and thoroughly kissed me again.

I was suddenly keenly aware of how quiet it was outside. The singing had stopped. The drums were silent, waiting for the new drummers. As Greg's tongue swept over mine, I realized we were finally alone in the darkness. I smiled against his lips, holding him tightly—loving him as he shuddered in my arms.

I was home.

GOAT BOY

Jack Fritscher

Volume = Radius x pi x Length
Radius = Circumference ÷ 2
Volume = Circumference ÷ 2 x Length

On the morning of his eighteenth birthday, Giles flipped his hot dick out on the Formica top of the kitchen table. The farmhouse was empty. He was alone. He was stark naked. His balls hung low against the cool table. He ran one hand up his flat belly. He reached down with his other hand and teased the tip of his big cock lying like a white sausage on the red Formica.

His soft tube steak rolled like a beached moby dick. It was alive. It had a mind of its own. It rolled to the left. Then the right. It pushed its head snub into the Formica, hardened, and marched nose onward, untouched by human hands. It had a mind of its own.

He touched the tip again. A pearl of clear gleat wet his finger. He rolled the juice around the head of his meat that was slithering thick and bulbous across the family dinner table. Blue veins wrapped around under white skin. He felt the blood rushing from all over his strong young body to fill the full width and length of his engorging cock.

It was an experiment.

He placed both hands on the white mounds of his hard butt. He pushed into the table. He wanted to make his cock crawl by itself, un-helped by his hands, across the table.

The experiment was working.

The wet head dribbled its whale's trail of juice, lubing the way for the thick shaft to follow. He was almost fully hard. He pushed his hips into the table. The salt and pepper shakers rocked back and forth. He fucked the table again. His cock took to the pressure and hardened out to its full length.

Within reach, on top of the refrigerator, he had stashed his dad's sixteen-foot retractable tape measure. It was silver with a yellow circle that read *Stanley. Powerlock II.* It was the kind of tape measure you pull out and then push a button to make it retract like sharp lightning.

His teencock lay big and hard and ripe on the table.

He reached for the tape measure and set its butt against the blond curly hair of his crotch. The case felt cool against the side of his cock.

Carefully, he pulled the ruler from its case.

One inch. Two. Three.

His dick pulsed and surged on further across the table.

Four. Five. Six.

He knew that was as long as his prick-record had been on his twelfth birthday. He ran his tongue across his lips. He pulled another inch out of the tape. Then another. He touched his chin to his chest, looking down the length of his slender body. His cock jumped when he saw the number nine appear black on the

yellow tape. His balls ached for his hand to cup them. His dick
begged for a spit-wet hand to stroke it. Heat flushed his face. He
tossed his head up like a wild young stallion. He sighed and bit
his lips. He looked down at the table. He looked down at his
dick. He looked down at the tape measure.

He had more meat to go.

He felt the way he had felt during the Olympics: seeing what
it meant to go for the gold. He touched the end of the tape and
inched it out slowly, one-fourth, one-half—and then the heavy
look of the number ten riding on the yellow tape moving slowly
out from the case. "A perfect ten," he said. And he smiled, pulling the tape just a fraction more, out to the very tip of his rock-
hard prick. "A perfect ten and then some."

He was ten-plus inches long and nearly nine inches around.
He was glad his geometry teacher had taught him how to figure
mass volume of a cylinder:

$$Volume = Circumference \div 2 \ x \ Length$$

He looked down at the table.

He sported a hefty forty-five cubic inches of dick.

The sight of his meat made him crazy. He wanted to shout
out the news of what he packed away inside his nylon running
shorts, inside his red Speedos, inside his jeans. He wanted his
dad to know. He wanted his mom to know.

He took his dick in both his hands and worked them up and
down the shaft. He marched around the kitchen. He was a teenage boy in heat. Alone at home. Naked in the afternoon. Crazy
with lust at the size of his own meat. Jumping up and down. Making his blood-heavy rod bob up and down and feel so good.

He ran his hands across his tight chest. He rubbed his pert
nipples. He flexed his belly and his butt. He gyrated his hips

and revolved his big dick in wide circles. He was eighteen and crazy and loving it. He had the biggest dick he had ever seen. Bigger than any dick hanging down all wet and soapy in the high-school shower room.

He slapped his pud on the table, then harder in his hand. He gritted his teeth and stroked himself up to the edge of shooting his hot load of teenseed all over the kitchen floor.

He fell back against the sink. He turned on the faucet. He filled a glass with water. He drank half of it to slake his thirst, then he plunged his dick deep into the glass.

The water that was left forced its way around his rod and out the neck of the glass. For a moment, he thought he had gone too far. His dick, three-quarters deep, looked like pressed meat inside the glass tumbler. A slight panic. A tug. He stuck his finger in between his dick and the edge of the glass. He broke the suction. He twisted the glass. He twisted his cock. Pure pleasure. He pulled the glass slowly away from his groin.

He spied a butter dish on the kitchen cabinet. He scooped up three fingersfull and shoved the butter into the glass tumbler. He lay back on the cool kitchen floor, jacking off his dick into the glass that held the heat of his meat. He fucked his hips up into the glass. He held the base of his dick with one hand and pounded his big pud into the glass with his other hand.

He was a one-man orgy.

Fuckcrazy.

Cumcrazy! His big balls ached. They bounced up against the glass and his hand. They bounced against the cool floor. He breathed deeply, caught his breath, settled back, changed his pace, and slowly, slowly, began the slow fuck of his dick, pulling the slippery, sucking glass up nearly to the head of his dick, then sliding it back down, till the tender head of his meat pushed against the bottom of the glass; pulling the glass up, up, up, then

off his dick; teasing his cockhead with the smooth rim of the
glass; feeling the butter melt, running down the shaft, through
his blond pubes, across his balls, and into the crack of his ass.

He was making a mess and he loved it.

He licked one finger and stuck it up his asshole. He suction-
pumped the glass up and down his upstanding cock. He writhed
on the floor. His hands smeared the butter across his fresh young
body.

He felt pinned on his back by wrestlers from the senior var-
sity team. He closed his eyes and imagined their weight pressing
down on his hard dick held tight inside a jockstrap inside his
wrestling singlet.

He raised himself up from the kitchen floor to a wrestling
bridge position: palms of hands and feet on the floor, small of his
back arched up, his head hanging down between his arms, his
flat belly curved up toward the ceiling, his erect cock pointing
straight up into the cool air.

He held the position that Coach Blue had taught him.

He thrust his dick up higher and higher. The ten inches of his
meat vaulted above his pumping arched body. His dick drove
ceilingward.

Small pearls of hot juice squeezed out the tight opening in the
big tip, and teared down the mushroom corona of the big head,
hanging for a moment on the lip of the crown, then sliding fast
down the blue-veined tracks of the shaft.

He ached with pleasure hoisting the ten inches high above his
body. Sweat broke out under the glaze of butter.

He slid slowly to the floor. He panted. His belly heaved. His
balls ached. His dick stretched out even above the double-grasp
of both his hands fisting his meat, hard, up and down, smash-
masturbating himself to a frenzy.

He entered his final heat.

Greased and sweating he rose from the floor.

He felt dirty and he loved the feeling. He locked his eyes on some mid-distance point like a jock ready to take the high jump. He felt wild and he liked the feeling. It was his birthday and he liked the feeling: eighteen, packing a real sweet ten inches.

He could do what the fuck he wanted. No one would know. No one would ever know.

He felt his fresh load oozing toward the head of his throbbing dick. He felt that mean green trigger in the back of his head begin to click.

He walked to the refrigerator. It was clear now. The vision was in his head. It was his birthday. The birthday boy could do anything. And he knew what he would do.

He felt his load building. He slammed his hard cock against the refrigerator. He opened the door. He pulled out the special meatloaf he knew his mom wanted to surprise him with at his birthday dinner.

He knew he could do it. He knew he would do it.

He put the red meatloaf on the floor.

He bit his lip, grinning at the splendid joke, and slid to his knees.

He straddled the meatloaf between his slick young thighs.

He dragged his balls through the ketchup circle on top of the meat.

Then he raised up halfway and with both hands stroked his big ten-incher no more than a dozen strokes before he came, arching his head back, howling like a banshee, shooting his load across the meatloaf, rising up, falling back, then falling forward on his hands and toes, pumping out pushups, hard-on into the hamburger, until every last spasm of his teenage body drained the seed from his dick, until finally he lay exhausted, spent, drained, and happy across the meatloaf.

He dozed. He slept the dreams of angels. He didn't recall for how long. Finally, he woke with a start.

He knew what he must do.

He cleaned the kitchen floor, washed the glass tumbler, and put away his father's tape measure.

He reconstructed the meatloaf, putting it and its extra ingredient back into the refrigerator.

Then he showered, ready to greet his father when he came in from the fields and his mother when she came home with birthday presents in her hands.

OPENING DAY AT THE COUNTY FAIR

J. M. Snyder

About the only thing that happens here in Boydton County is the annual fair. The first week in October everyone turns out at the fairgrounds, their livestock and crops in tow. There are cattle auctions, hog-calling contests, funnel cakes, chitlins, and Best of Show ribbons given out for everything from largest cucumber to fattest sow. On any given day there's maybe five hundred people all told, jostling for a place inside the split rail fence that cuts the grounds out from the surrounding fields. Believe me, that's a crowd around these parts, and all the pickups and John Deeres tear up the dirt tracks that lead into the fairgrounds something fierce. When the fair committee manages to wrangle someone famous to stop on by, the mud and the muck just gets worse. Few years back, they had that guy who played Deputy Enos on *The Dukes of Hazzard*, and you'd have thought it was Boss Hogg himself. This year my sister Jolene heard it might be Toby Keith, but I think she heard wrong because there's no *way* the county could cough up the money to bring someone big like him here. I mean, really.

The day the fair's set to open, Jolene wakes me up at four thirty, just before dawn. Since it's still dark out at this hour, it takes her several minutes to rouse me out of sleep. Barely opening my eyes, I groan, "God, Jo. It's too early."

"Come *on*," she mutters, keeping her voice down so she won't wake our folks. "Jesse, you said you'd drive me to the fair. Missy's outside and *waiting* already." Missy is Jolene's prize pig—she won four ribbons three years back and Jo's been making money selling her offspring at every fair since. Vaguely I remember telling her that I'd give her a ride to the fairgrounds, but right at this moment I can't for the life of me imagine why.

When I don't stir, Jolene shoves my bed and hisses, "Jesse!" Then she shucks off her sneakers and clambers on top of my covers, nothing but pointy elbows and skinny legs that poke at me in unpleasant places. Rising to her feet, she stomps about my mattress, narrowly missing my hands and face. "Wake up," she chants in time with her steps. "Wake up, wake up, wake up." I curl into a fetal position and squeeze my eyes shut, but what's the use? She's won. Still, I hold out until she stops moving and threatens, "I'll tell Pa."

Only then do I stretch awake. The last thing I need is my father in here, towering over my bed with his hard eyes, asking in that dangerously low voice of his how a hardworking man like him managed to sire a lazy do-nothing freeloader like me. I'll never be good enough for him, I've learned that lesson over the last twenty years, but that's never kept me from trying. As I kick Jolene off the bed, I yawn and tell her, "I'm up already." I hate the triumphant grin on her face—little sisters sure know how to get under your skin. Running a hand through my close-cropped hair, I ask, "You load Missy up yet?"

"She won't go up the ramp for me," Jolene admits. "I got the piglets boxed in but Pa said to come get you since it's your truck. He's got Mamma's veggie crates already stacked up by the back tire, too, waiting for you."

Suddenly I feel the weight of the coming week heavy on my shoulders. Loading the truck, then driving slowly over back country roads for an hour to get to the fairgrounds, unloading the truck, uncrating the vegetables and the pigs and sitting in the bed of my pickup for long, hot hours watching people pick over both. Six days of that shit. When I was little, the fair used to be as big as Christmas for me, but this early in the morning I don't have the energy to get that worked up anymore. "God," I moan, rubbing my face with both hands.

Because I'm not moving fast enough for her, Jolene kicks me in the shin.

By the time we get to the fairgrounds, there's already a line of battered trucks edging the fence. My mother's half-brother Gary stands at the open gate, waving vendors on through. He's county administrator and since it's an elected position, he makes sure that he's seen. The day has begun to brighten, but the sky is white from a faint haze that hangs above the grounds like wet laundry. As I pull up to the gates, I lean out the window and holler, "Looks like rain."

"It'll hold," Gary tells me. With a glance at Jolene in the bed of my truck, he adds, "Pigsty's in the back, you know the way."

I inch the truck along the main thoroughfare, one foot on the brake pedal as we crawl along behind other trucks between lines of vendors setting up their booths. There's a tractor somewhere up ahead, I hear the ragged engine churn in the rising heat, and people dart across the strip, dodging between the trucks as they chase after children or livestock that have managed to get away.

Twice I hit the steering wheel in frustration but I don't bother to use the horn—wouldn't do any good. Instead I glare out the window at anyone who dares to meet my gaze and egg the truck on in little jolts that make Jolene tap angrily against the cab's back window. I've been up for hours and haven't even eaten yet, it's getting hot already, the stench of livestock permeates the air, I'm in a sour mood, and I'm thinking that next year there's no *way* I'm doing this shit again—when for the first time in ages I see someone I don't know.

He's a young man, about my age, shirt off to expose pale skin that hasn't seen the sun all summer and a back that glistens with sweat as he hammers a couple of two-by-fours into a booth. Light hair the color of bailed hay falls to his shoulders, and I stare at his slender frame, memorizing the flex of thin muscles across narrow shoulder blades. It's Mrs. Colton's booth he's working on—she stands to one side with her hands on her ample hips, cans of preserves around her feet. When she sees me looking, she calls out, "Y'all come by for some of my jelly, you hear? I got something new you'll want to try."

"So I see," I reply. That earns me a smirk from the stranger. Encouraged, I add, "What's his name?"

Mrs. Colton doesn't get my drift, thank god. "This here's Ruddy Johnson's boy. Davis?" Instead of a sideways glance this time he turns to look at me, eyebrows arched and with a suggestive grin. "Jesse Sadler, his sister Jolene. My, that Missy has some size to her."

Davis. His eyes challenge me to turn away but I can't, I'm drawn to him like a moth to a flame and I imagine lying beneath him, pinned into submission under that steady gaze. In my mind I can see just how dusky my skin would look alongside his white flesh; I can taste his sweat, smell his scent, almost feel how firm his body would be against my hands. As I stare, he gives me a quick wink that makes my dick go from mildly interested to "Hello!" in one heartbeat. I'm so caught up in him that I don't even realize the traffic has stopped moving until I bump into the truck in front of us. Jolene pounds on the glass behind me hard enough to rattle it in my ear.

"Sorry!" I holler, cringing at the look the driver ahead gives me in his side-view mirror. *God.* Davis laughs, the sound boyish and so bright that it makes me want to sink down into my seat and die of embarrassment. As the line of trucks starts to move forward, I duck my head and hide the side of my face behind my hand so I won't be tempted to look his way again.

When we reach the pigsty, Jolene jumps down from the bed of the truck and wants to know, "What'd you run up on Bubba's bumper for?"

"You're only eleven," I tell her. "You wouldn't understand."

"I'm twelve," she counters. "I know more than you think." I shrug her comment off, but she warns, "And you best hope Pa don't see you making eyes at any boys."

All right, so maybe she *is* a bit more perceptive than I thought.

Ruddy Johnson is the only person I know of who left the county and didn't drop off the face of the earth. He still comes back once a year for the county fair—he's a contractor now, works out of the state capital, but he and Gary went to high school together and folks don't mind him coming down, seeing as he was once one of their own. If I'd known Ruddy had a son like Davis, I might have let Gary talk me into hiring on to one of his work crews earlier this summer.

As my sister goes about uncrating the pigs, I lean against the side of my truck and wonder how long I can stall putting our booth together in the hopes that Davis will eventually drift down this way to help. I squint back along the main strip, but I can't pick him out from the people milling about. When Jolene tells me to get a move on, I flick the toothpick I'm chewing at her and haul one crate of tomatoes out of the truck, set it on the ground at my feet, then take another look around. Still no sign of Davis. I can't believe he's not somewhere thinking about me right now. Lord knows I wasn't the only one staring.

I pull out two more crates, these loaded with unshucked corn, and manage to make enough room to get Missy down. Maybe I was wrong about the guy, but just thinking about that wink he gave me sets my blood on fire. As I unload the truck, my mind is tucked in some fantasy world where Davis stretches above me like the sky, his smile the sun. My motions are automatic, my thoughts spun out in a whirl, and I don't hear the approaching footsteps or sense I'm no longer alone until a voice behind me says, "I was beginning to wonder when you'd get to work."

The crate I'm holding falls from my hands and breaks when it hits the ground, spilling turnip greens across the muddy grass. It's him, Davis, standing so close that the greens cover the tops of his sneakers. "Damn," I sigh, nervous now that he's right up on me. He's thinner than I reckoned, wiry, with a strong jaw and light blue eyes that look almost see-through. His hair wisps in dry, sunburnt strands, the front of it pulled back in a tight pony-tail to keep it off his face. There's something randy about him, almost carnal, that hints at long afternoons twined together in the hayloft, strong fingers slipping into tight wet places, tongues hot on hidden flesh. Trying to push that thought out of my head, I sink to my knees to gather up the turnip greens and find myself eye level with his crotch. *Oh my god.*

Davis raises one eyebrow in interest. "Jesse, is it?" he asks, shifting his weight from one foot to the other to thrust his hips out at me. "I came by to see if you wanted me for anything."

Right this moment, staring past the slight bulge in his jeans and up the smooth expanse of his taut, hairless chest, I can imagine half a dozen different ways I want him. But before I can answer, he squats beside me and starts to scoop up the greens I'm neglecting. "Sorry about this," he says. "You need some help putting up your booth?" As if he's been talking about *that* all along. The hands that rub over mine beneath the turnip greens say otherwise.

I manage to find my voice. "Sure," I tell him, then thinking maybe I should say something more, I add, "Davis. That's an odd name. Ruddy's your pa?"

With a nod, he admits, "Davis is my middle name." He gathers up the greens, my hands stuck in the bundle, so I stand when he does to keep him from letting go. "It's better than Jeff, let me tell you. I used to be J.D. when I was younger. Some people still call me that. You any relation to that race car driver?"

He means Elliott Sadler—I get asked that a lot. The truth is no, but I shrug like maybe. He thrusts the greens into my arms and then wipes his hands on his hips, a move that pulls his jeans tight across his groin. "You don't talk much, do you?" he asks, bending down again to pick out two boards from the nearby stack. "My dad couldn't make it this year, so I'm stuck constructing all these booths. How about a hand?" He's moving too fast for me, running from one thought to the next with the quickness of a silverfish, but when he holds out one of the boards, I drop the turnip greens onto the open tailgate and take it, eager to keep up. "You hold it steady," Davis tells me, "and I'll hammer it in. What do you say?"

"Are we talking about the booth?" I ask.

Davis leers at me over his shoulder. "We're talking about wood. Where do you want me to put it?"

My mouth goes dry with lust and when I speak, my voice

barely makes it above a whisper. "Put what?" The booth? The
wood he's holding? His dick? I don't know about the first two
but I've got an idea where I'd like that last one to go. "You mean
the booth, right?"

Davis just laughs, a delicious sound that washes over me like
a summer breeze. "What do *you* think I mean?" he asks.

I'd really love to find out.

After our booth is up and Davis has moved on to the next ven-
dor, leaving me with aching balls and his promise to return when
he gets the chance, I set out as much of the vegetables as I can
and stack the empty crates in the back of my truck. The gates
open at ten, and for the first two hours, I'm on my feet hag-
gling with customers, trading the crops for cans of jam or preserves, pocketing payments and making change. I keep an eye on
Jolene but she's better at this than me, and by the time noon rolls
around, she's sold all of her piglets and gained two baby chicks
in addition to a fistful of dollars. Her fat sow Missy wallows
half-hidden in hot mud, but she's the biggest pig at the fair and it
looks like she might bring home another ribbon this year. When
Jolene's piglets are gone, she climbs into the back of my truck
and starts up a steady stream of chatter that I tune out while I
work. When the first rush finally ebbs away, I plop down on the
tailgate with a sigh. "You could help out here a bit," I tell her.

Jolene shakes her ponytail back with a haughty air. "Pa
said—"

I cut her off. "Pa ain't here." To keep her from arguing further, I pull one foot up on the tailgate, wrap my arms around my
knee, and hide my face in my arms. Sweat drips down the back
of my neck, behind my ears, under my arms, tracing intimate
lines across my body. For the first time since he left, I let myself
think of Davis. My own breath sounds close and harsh in the

scant darkness created by my crossed arms, but I close my eyes and there he is, that suggestive smile toying around the edges of his mouth. I recall the way he moved as he set up my booth, but in my mind I'm bold this time and when his back is to me, I step up behind him, ease my arms around his narrow waist, slip my hands into the front pockets of his jeans and rub against the hardness I find there. I press my face against his moist, hot back and breathe in his heady scent, a manly mix of musk and soap and sweat that turns me on something fierce. He backs up, ass arched into my crotch as I hug him to me, my lips trailing tiny kisses around his neck and along the rigid shelf of his collarbone. One of my hands encircles his erection through the pocket—in my fantasy he doesn't have on underwear. My kisses move lower, down his back now, over his shoulder blades and along the nubs of his spine, my hands pushing into his pockets until his pants start to slide down out of the way. I'm licking along the small of his back, where he has a tiny Chinese character tattooed at the base of his spine, and my tongue barely eases between the mounds of his fleshy buttocks... Jolene calls my name. I replay that daydream, starting at the spot where his tailbone ends, licking down the crevice of his ass, and she calls me again. A customer or something, I don't know, but my jeans cut across the start of my own erection with a sweet pain and I'm not ready to get back to the real world just yet, so I tell her, "Handle it, will you?"

With an exasperated huff, she jumps down from the truck, one small foot catching me in the hip as she passes by. I don't have the energy to fight with her right now. Where was I? Oh yes, tasting my way down damp flesh to the trembling, puckered prize beneath—

Something icy presses against the back of my neck, so cold that it takes my breath away. I jerk my head up, ready to lay into

Jolene for messing with me, only to see that Davis has found me again. He holds a can of Coke out to me, still wet from the cooler. "Thirsty?" he asks. I take the soda without comment, not trusting myself to speak. It's hard to mesh the naked image of him in my mind's eye with the living, breathing boy beside me. He leans against the side of my truck, so nonchalant, as if he has no clue what I'm thinking when I look his way. "So," he asks, "what do you guys do around here for fun?"

I take a swallow from the can and shrug. "This is about it," I admit. A look around at the fair in full swing and I see just how lame it must appear to someone like him. "Sorry if it's got you bored stiff."

"Oh, I'm stiff all right." Maybe he's thinking the same as me after all. But he'll probably try to play that off somehow, pretend he's not talking about what I think he's talking about, and I'm waiting for that laugh of his to ease the tension between us when he reaches out and smoothes one finger down the length of my arm. His touch is light, ticklish, and he watches the tip of his finger as it curves around my elbow and swings up to dust under the short sleeve of my T-shirt. I watch too, waiting, my lower lip caught bloodless between my teeth. His finger feels like a feather on my skin, barely there, but then he presses hard against a freckle and when I glance up at him, he's looking back. "Let's go somewhere," he whispers. My sister's busy with a customer at the front of the booth and can't overhear us, but Davis keeps his voice low and intimate. "Just you and me. What do you say?"

I want to say yes, I want to shout it out at the top of my lungs, but this isn't my folks' barn in the lower field, this is the county fair, and with Jolene around, there's nowhere we can be alone. Unsure, I start, "Where..."

Davis nods toward the front of the truck, and for a moment

I think he means for us to get in the cab. How private is that? But then I see the split rail fence and the wave of tall grass growing beyond the edges of the fairgrounds. "Out there?" I want to know.

In lieu of a reply he takes my wrist, his hand slipping easily into mine as he helps me off the tailgate. Over my shoulder I call out, "Hold down the fort, Jo. I'll be back."

We only take two steps toward the fence before my sister cuts in front of me, blocking the way. "Oh no, mister," she says with an angry shake of her head. "My job was the pigs and they're all gone so don't try to dump the crops on me, too. Where y'all going anyway? Don't you dare run off and leave me here. I'll tell Pa."

"Listen," I say, leaning down to look her in the eye. Davis tugs on my hand but I hold him back. "You might not believe me now, Jolene, but one day you're going to bring home a boy that Pa's not going to like." I don't mention that our father won't like any boy she brings home—let her find that out for herself. She gives me a wounded look, lip pooched out like she thinks I might be lying, but she's giving me a chance. "Trust me, once you get a little older, there will be plenty of times when you're gonna want to get away with someone and you're gonna be like, 'Jesse, can you cover for me here?' And what do you think I'm gonna say?"

"Where are you going?" she asks again, petulant.

I point out past the fence and tell her, "Just over there, I promise. If you need me, just holler. But you did a bang-up job with those piggies, Jo, and I know you can sell the hell out of some vegetables if you want to. What do you say?"

Jolene glares at the field as if hoping it'll burst into flame. Davis's hand is starting to sweat against mine, and he gives me a pleading look that she doesn't see. I'm just about to say fine,

she wins, I'll ache for this boy for the rest of my *life* just because she's too damn stubborn to cut me some slack, when she
sighs. "Fine," she grumbles. She pouts at me, then at Davis, then
whips her ponytail back with a defiant shake of her head, but
she steps aside to let me pass. Without waiting for her to change
her mind, I let Davis pull me toward the fence. As I'm climbing over I glance back, but Jolene's already at the booth again,
weighing out a bag of butter beans for another customer.

The grass grows right up to the edge of the fence, a wild mix
of buffalo grass, switchgrass, and tall fescue, with some late-
blooming wild alfalfa sprouts purpling the field. It's thigh high
in most places, and as Davis and I move through it, a fine cloud
of seeds and dust and insects rises up around us. After a dozen
yards or so, the land slopes gently to a small ridge, then tumbles
down into a gully thick with crabgrass and poison ivy. When
Davis stops, kicking through the grass to find a good spot to
sit, I look back to make sure I can still see Jolene. From here
the front of my truck hides the booth, and I'm just about to say
maybe we should move a little one way or the other so I can
keep an eye on my sister when Davis falls back against the slope
and pulls me down with him. "Here?" I ask, rolling onto my
back. My stomach flutters as his hand tickles above the waistband of my jeans. The grass scratches my neck and arms, and
rises around us to block out everything but the sky and Davis
propped above me. The crowded fairgrounds sound like nothing
more than wind rustling through fields a million miles away.

"Here," Davis breathes. He lies beside me, his stomach
pressed against my side, and leans down to nuzzle my ear. When
he speaks, his words fill me up inside as if they're my own
thoughts in his voice. "Where should we begin?"

Gingerly I reach up and touch his face. He leans his cheek
against my palm, then kisses my wrist. I guide him toward me,

my mouth eager for his, my tongue licking along his upper lip before delving inside. He tastes sweet, sugary, like the soda he's been drinking, and his tongue massages mine with an urgency that presses our lips together in a velvety crush. My hand fists in his short ponytail, pulling him further toward me, and he pushes me to the ground with the strength of his kiss, his arms cradling me as he holds me down, his legs straddling my hips, his body covering mine.

Through the double layer of our jeans, our cocks rub together, thrusting against each other as if locked in an ancient battle. His kiss becomes lustful, his hands rough in my hair, his body unyielding in its desire for mine. Somehow we break apart long enough to pull my shirt up over my head and I gasp as his teeth close over one hard nugget of a nipple, biting it erect. "God," I sigh, holding his head in both hands as he nips his way down my stomach. His tongue licks into my navel, then he bites at the pliant skin, his fingers now at my waist and unzipping my jeans. My legs part as he moves lower, my knees rising on either side of him as he kisses the length of hair that leads into my crotch and then pulls down my pants and briefs. As if responding to the sudden sunlight and autumn air, my dick stands up from its patch of thick curls, pointing at Davis like an accusation. I raise my legs into the air, sure he's going to tug the jeans off completely, but he only gets them down to my knees before he crawls into the space between, mouth open, tongue licking out to taste the head of my dick.

With my legs on his shoulders, Davis kneels before me and traces the length of my shaft from tip to base with one long lick. As he takes my balls into his mouth, sucking the soft skin and rolling them around with that maddening tongue of his, I arch my hips up to meet him. He releases my aching sac and moves lower, licking the smooth, tender skin before pressing against my tight hole. "God," I gasp again, fists full of grass as he rims me, his tongue dancing between my buttocks. I work my muscles, trying to draw him in, but he stays just out of reach. Then he's back at my cock again, rubbing the spongy tip against the roof of his mouth as his saliva cools down my length. Something's building inside of me, something untamed, unfettered, and I want to scream out at the world all the frustration and anxiety he's whipping up in me. I want him to take me, god please, just lay into me until I'm left raw and bared and exhausted. His touch is driving me to the brink of insanity, his kisses push me over the edge. "Fuck me," I plead, "please, *please*. God, Davis, don't make me beg. Just *do* it already, will you?"

He laughs, *laughs*, I can't believe it. "Don't like this?" he asks, and one finger slips up my ass to bump my desire another notch or two higher. As he moves inside me I try to hold him in, I want more and my cock is throbbing for release but I won't give in, not yet. His mouth is on me again, this time taking me in completely, until his lips kiss the base of my shaft and his mussed hair tickles my lower belly. He shoves deep inside me, sending bursts of pleasure tingling up my spine and down my legs, igniting every nerve ending I have. I raise one hand to my mouth and bite the fleshy pad below my thumb, bite down hard against the sensations flooding my body. I feel him everywhere, in my ass, my cock, my heart. When he pulls his finger out and lets my erection slip free from his lips, I bite down harder and barely manage to choke back a sob.

Eyes shut, I try to steady my breathing. I'm close to release, *god* so close, but I hear the telltale sound of his zipper, hear him grunt as he tears open a condom, and I know this is it, here it comes, "Please." My voice is a broken, tearful plea. "Davis..."

"Coming right up," he promises. I hear him shuck off his pants and then he's back, hunching his shoulders to squeeze into the tight space between my knees. As he climbs over me, one hand on either side of my head, I rest my jean-sheathed lower legs on his narrow hips. The wet tip of his dick nudges against my quivering hole, pokes at me once or twice, then finally, *finally* plunges inside.

He shoves in as far as he'll go and stops. Above me his face eclipses the world, his eyes so clear it seems as if I'm looking through them to the sky beyond. He stares down at me, forcing me to look at him, holding my attention while he's so deep inside and then, incredibly, he gives a little thrust and moves in just an inch or two more. Pressure builds inside me, a breathless wait—his gaze refuses to let me turn away. Another tiny thrust, and another, and another, and just when I think I can't take any more, he's in too deep and I'm going to explode if he goes in any further, he pulls out half an inch. An eternity passes; I hold my breath and wait for him to thrust in again with those little tiny fucks that wind me up tight inside. As he moves within me, his mouth closes over mine in a tender kiss.

I feel shattered afterward, a scarecrow torn into pieces and left scattered around the fields. Davis holds me close, kissing the back of my neck as he murmurs my name. My pants are still around my knees, my shirt somewhere in the grass nearby, and Davis is buck naked behind me, nothing on but that used condom still dangling from his limp member and lying wet between my thighs. I try to smooth out the grass imprints on his arms but the pink flesh stays indented. The fairgrounds still sound so far away, but the sun has begun to slant along the fields. I lace my fingers through his, hug his arms against my chest—I want to lie here forever, trapped in the circle of his embrace.

But footsteps swishing through the grass near the fence remind us that we're not alone. Reluctantly I sit up, dust the grass

out of my hair, off my shoulders, arms, legs and back. I don't look
at Davis as we dress, silent, each lost in his own thoughts. As he
leads the way back to the fair, I reach out to brush the grass off
his butt. His hand catches mine. "Copping a feel?" he asks, one
eyebrow cocked salaciously. He raises my hand to his lips, kisses
the tips of my fingers, then lets me go. "You here all week?"

I thought he'd never ask. Not to seem too eager, though,
I shrug like maybe and he punches me playfully in the arm.
"Don't be like that," he says. "I got bite marks underneath my
chin where you sank your teeth in, Jesse. You liked it."

"I didn't say I didn't." The next time he looks up, I duck
down to see under his chin. Damned if there isn't a faint red
welt, and he's got a hickey coming up along his jawline. I point
it out. "That's gonna be pretty."

We've reached the fence. Davis leans back against it, grabs
the belt loops on the front of my jeans and tugs me toward him.
"Davis," I warn. We're behind my truck and mostly out of sight,
but this is a small county and I surely don't need this getting
around. Still, his skin looks smooth and creamy, and I can't stop
myself from trailing a hand down his flat belly to hook in the
front of his jeans. He's watching me with an unnerving stare,
waiting for me to answer his previous question. "I'll be here,"
I tell him.

He gives me a sunny smile. "Me too. I'm staying with Gary—"

"Stay with me," I say. It slips out before I can think to stop
it, and the way his face lights up, I hate myself when I have to
add, "Only I still live with my folks. Gary's my half-uncle, so
Momma'll put you up, but Pa won't cotton to us getting it on
in his house."

Davis's smile twists into a sly grin, and his eyes sparkle mis-
chievously. With a tug on my jeans, he pulls me closer and I
stumble into him, my nipples stiffening where they brush against

his. In my ear he whispers, "Then we'll just have to go out-side."

And suddenly six days doesn't seem long enough for this year's fair.

BAREBACK RIDER

Michael Bracken

Every time the rodeo came to town, the local bars were crowded with hard-muscled men clad in tight-fitting Wranglers, snap-button shirts, low-heeled ropers, sweat-stained Stetsons, and belt buckles the size of dinner plates. Following the rodeo circuit were the wannabes and the used-to-bes, the groupies and the clingers-on, and they crowded into the bars along with the cowboys and the rodeo employees. Included in every crowd in every bar were the locals, the men and women who brushed against masculine greatness for one long weekend and lived on the adrenaline rush for the following twelve months.

Justin Longacre, a bareback rider who frequently finished in the money, rolled into town in his extended cab dually the day before the rodeo's first event, booked himself a room at the Motel 6 just down the road from the coliseum, and began to prowl the local bars. Justin had the sinewy build of a man who had been stretched tight and held together by sheer determination. Unlike other bareback riders, the abuse he had endured seemed negligible: he'd smashed his face against the skull of a particularly spirited bronc, leaving his nose with a flat spot just above his nostrils, and a bad dismount had broken his left leg, giving him a barely perceptible limp.

In each of the bars Justin visited, men bought his drinks and women sidled up to him, offering themselves as if they were breeder cows. He always politely tasted the drinks and thanked the women for their attention before moving on, riding the local alcohol circuit the way he rode the southwest rodeo circuit.

In one bar near the Interstate, a well-lit place that catered to upscale out-of-towners, he had to explain to a buxom young coed what a bareback rider did.

"It's just me and the horse," he said. "No saddle, no stirrups, no reins, just a leather rigging that looks like a suitcase handle on a strap."

He explained to the attentive coed that cowboys grab the handle with one hand and throw their free hand in the air to keep from touching themselves or the horse during the ride. The cowboy must mark out when the horse leaves the chute, making sure that both spurs touch the bronc's shoulders. Then the cowboy spurs the horse from shoulder to rigging, doing his best to score points based on his strength, control, and spurring action during the eight-second ride.

"That sounds crazy," the coed said.

Justin had heard another rider describe it once and he'd repeated the description ever since. "It's the hardest eight-second ride on earth," Justin said, "like riding a jackhammer one-handed."

The coed lost interest when Justin failed to produce a room key or a desire to pay her bar tab and she wandered away in search of a softer touch. Justin resumed his cruise through the central Texas town's ample supply of watering holes until he found himself straddling a red leatherette stool and leaning against the worn wood of a bar in a dark hole downtown, about as far away from rodeo people as he could get in distance and ideology.

"The rodeo must be back in town," said a soft-skinned young blond who settled onto the stool next to Justin.

"Yep."

"I thought I smelled cow flop."

Justin looked the young man over. Steven Pitt had the physique of an office worker, gym-toned but without the hard edges that only backbreaking outdoor work provided. He wore a dark suit, his rep tie still knotted at the collar. His close-cropped hair had been styled recently and his fingernails manicured. The faint aroma of expensive cologne settled around him.

"You a real cowboy, or a reject from the Village People?"

Justin stared into the younger man's eyes. "I'm a bareback rider."

Steven looked the cowboy up and down, as if searching for hidden meanings. "Why?"

"I like the risk," Justin explained. "Using a saddle just doesn't feel the same."

The young man considered for a moment, and then ordered two shots and beers. After the pug-faced bartender slid the drinks to them, Steven asked, "You in town long?"

"Just as long as the rodeo's here," Justin said. "Then I move on."

"Just like that?" asked the young blond. "No commitments?"

"I'm just looking for a good buck," Justin said. "I ride and I move on."

Steven lowered his voice and leaned into Justin. "You want to ride me?"

The question hung in the air unanswered until the two men finished their drinks. Justin followed Steven out of the bar and two blocks away to the bedroom of a third-floor walk-up apartment. Under Justin's watchful eye, Steven stripped off all of his clothes except his tie, revealing a smooth, hairless body tanning-bed tanned the color of honey. Justin grunted his approval and peeled off his own clothes, revealing his own redneck tan. His face, neck, hands, and arms from mid-bicep down had the beef jerky color of a man who worked outdoors, while the rest of his hard body remained pasty white because it never saw sunlight. A dark patch of untamed hair at the juncture of his thighs provided a nest for his thick cock and heavy balls.

Steven dropped to his knees on the carpet in front of Justin and took the cowboy's rapidly stiffening cock into his mouth. As his tongue circled Justin's glans, he cupped Justin's heavy scrotum in his hands and massaged the cowboy's testicles. Then he used his middle finger to stroke the sensitive spot behind Justin's scrotum.

Justin reached down and held the back of Steven's head, feeling the stiffness of the young man's perfectly arranged hair as he pumped his hips against Steven's face. Soon he exploded in the younger man's mouth, and Steven swallowed every drop. After the young blond licked Justin clean, he stood, dug through his nightstand for lubricant, and then handed the tube to Justin.

"Ride me," Steven whispered as he turned around and bent over his bed. He placed his hands on the down comforter to brace himself. "Ride me hard."

Justin squeezed a drop of lubricant onto his finger and then applied it to Steven's rectum, teasing the younger man's fancy by pressing the tip of his middle finger against the tight sphincter, but not entering him.

After Justin withdrew his finger, he pressed the head of his cock against Steven's lubricated sphincter, pressing forward until he entered him. Then he grabbed Steven's tie, pulling Steven's head back as he drove forward, burying his cock deep inside Steven. Justin threw his free hand into the air as he drew back and pressed forward again. And again.

And Steven bucked, forcing himself backward to meet each of Justin's powerful thrusts. As Justin continued pounding into him from behind, Steven reached down and took his own turgid penis into his fist. He pumped furiously, coming across his comforter as the tie tightened around his neck and only moments before Justin came inside him.

Justin had ridden Steven long and hard and well beyond the eight seconds that would be required in the rodeo arena the next afternoon, and he continued holding the younger man's tie in one hand until his penis stopped throbbing. Then he dismounted, pulling his cock away with a barely audible pop.

Steven collapsed on the bed, clawing at the tie until he loosened it from his neck. As soon as he caught his breath, Steven rolled over to watch the cowboy.

Justin dressed, dropped a rodeo guest pass on Steven's chest, and said, "If you want to see how a real man rides, come tomorrow."

Justin let himself out, walked to his truck, and returned to the Motel 6. He eased his dually between two full-sized pickups outfitted with expensive tow packages, bought a diet Dr Pepper from a machine near the motel office, and returned to his room to drink it. Then he showered and climbed into bed alone because he always slept alone.

The next afternoon, Justin completed his first eight-second ride with a respectable score in the low eighties, and the pickup men swooped in to pull him from the still-bucking horse. After they lowered him to the ground, Justin looked into the stands. As soon as he saw Steven watching him, Justin knew he had a few more good rides ahead of him that weekend. In every town, no matter how big or how small, Justin Longacre always found a good ride. Sometimes it was a horse named Diablo, Crazy Eight, or Snake Eyes, and sometimes it was a man named Brogan, or Charles, or Thad. Justin didn't care which it was because he always rode bareback.

He lived to take risks. It was the cowboy way.

WATERMELON MAN

Shane Allison

W hatchu doin' here? Tol' you tuh never come here."

The man veered around the table of gold-plated crosses, tennis bracelets and hoop earrings with his signature piece of watermelon, and pulled out a vacant lawn chair.

"Don't worry," he said. "I'll be gone befo' yuh mama come back." He smelled like dirt and rotten trash. Pink pearls of watermelon juice dripped from wrinkled, rough hands. "Where she at?"

"She went tuh church. I gotta watch th' table till she come back."

I hate this poor white trash flea market. The scent of funnel cakes frying fills my lungs. I'm only here 'cause Mama wanted to go to church. She keeps complaining about how she hasn't been in weeks

"So whatchu want?" The pepper from the watermelon made me sneeze.

"Bless ya," he said, spitting out black seeds.

Who puts pepper on watermelon? He was so country. I watched in disgust as he bit into the soft, red fruit. He was wet with sweat, sticky from the juice. The sharp smell of pepper lingered in hot heat. He was old enough to be my daddy. He'd been a good friend of Ma's since middle school. He was eating that melon like it was the last he'd ever have.

That's how he got the name. Watermelon Man.

He plucked two scented naps from a box of Wet Ones and wiped his hands clean of juice. A couple of old ladies fawned over anklets and dolphin necklaces. One said the jewelry was fake.

"Come ova t'night," he said.

"Cain't."

"Why?"

"Buzy."

"Doin' what?"

"None of yuh bizness, an' anotha thang, don't be callin' my house an' hangin' up. Ma's gon' fine out it's you. We got calla ID too, man."

"What um 'pose to do? It's been weeks an' I wanna see yuh."

"I toljuh' I'll let yuh know."

Ma rode up. It started to get busy. Thank fuckin' god.

"Well, well, well." She was dressed to the nines in her navy skirt suit, white gloves, and hat to match. She never goes to church without something on her head. Her hair has thinned because of that bad perm Terri put in it. He was as happy to see her as I was happy to be rescued from this loud-talking nut.

"You jus' comin' from church?" he asked.

"It was a good service," she said.

"Was it?"

"Yes g'ness."

I wandered off to the side of our table to assist a younger

woman interested in an anklet of cute little elephants. It didn't
fit, too damn tight.

"You might need a ten or an eleven."

Him and Ma went on about neighborhood pastors, the latest
flea market rumors.

"It's too tight. I cain't fasten it," she said. I wanted to say
it was because she had smoked hams for ankles, but I kept my
mouth shut. She placed the anklet back on the table. Examined
other pieces of jewelry while gradually walking off. I stared at
his arms glistening with sweat, the sweat trickling off his hairy
chest. He was a slouchy mess. I stared at his crotch, remembering the size. Sweaty and smelly beneath thin, swarthy skin
that blanketed the head. Over Ma's navy shoulder, I watched the
Rastafarian selling incense, Jamaican flags.

Watermelon Man with his white row of teeth. Dentures, jux-
taposed nicely against ominous skin. Every Saturday around this
time it got busy. I worked one end while Mama took care of
folks on the other. He pushed his trash can out of the corner,
started down the flea market aisle, sweeping up cigarette butts
and beer cans.

Ma made almost four hundred dollars off the X and O bracelets. She packed the last gold-plated necklace in a Rubbermaid
bend. I excused myself to the bathroom 'cause I'd drunk sodas
all day and my dick was full of piss for it. There was a toilet
over by one of the refreshment stands. The food cost too much
out here. Two dollars for a corn dog, five for a paper plate of
greasy cheese fries. We always brought sandwiches, drinks to
last till we went to the all-you-can-eat buffet. The bathroom
was filthy, reeking of pee. I pressed the dispenser for soap.
Empty and dry. The hot water tap was torn off leaving only the
cold to work. The stall was small, the trash can running over
with soiled, brown paper towels, balls of wet tissue. I unzipped

my jeans and forked out my dick. I stood over the toilet as a tongue of urine plopped in commode water. I couldn't help but think about him. My hands embracing his booty snug in denim days old. A dirty Southerner. I think of his privates in public. Piss poured and splashed as the door opened. He entered, letting in light. He startled me, Mama's junior high chum. Heavy breathing.

"Whatchu doin' in there?"

"What it look like? Takin' a piss." He stood outside my stall, peeked in over the wall. "Fuck you doin'?"

"I saw you lookin'."

"What?" I pretended not to know what he was talking about. I prayed he wouldn't try anything. Not with the sheriff in the office right outside. We ran the risk of getting caught. I tucked things back into rightful places.

"Hol' up." He jotted something on a torn piece of brown paper towel and handed it to me, his name and number and address written in crimson ink.

"Why you givin' me this?"

"Fo' when you get bored." His fingers were rough against my hand. I've never known hard work. Couldn't wait to git out of there. I rinsed my hands under that tongue of cold and dried them clean. I pretended I wasn't interested. I looked at his number. My head is a camera. My memory's a photograph. I took his number and tucked it in the pocket of my shirt. He was all I thought about as Ma and I sat down for Sunday dinner.

Days passed, the week was uneventful. Work and home pretty much. I was saving money to move, inhabit a place of my own, a place to throw parties, a pad to entertain. Love Mama, but we've had our share of late night fights. Sick of feeling like some kind of caged animal behind these barred windows, these ten-

inch impenetrable doors. A hundred more and I'd have enough.
I don't tell Ma what I wanna do: fame and fortune, a writer of
film and television. She'd think me silly.

He popped up on the porch one day with a bag of fruit. I opened
the verticals and there he was. He smiled pretty but that's not
why he came. I answered the door bare-chested wearing nothing
to cover me but boxers. Barely able to keep my dick secure.

"These fo' yuh Mama."

"She ain't here."

He stood at the door, black and sweaty, dressed in a red tee,
dirty Guess jeans, and dusty carpenter boots.

"Where she at?"

"She went to a revival." She's getting closer to God. Because
of the leaky roof, the unfinished work, Ma didn't like people
coming to the house.

"I tol' yuh Mama I would be brangin' these by. They navel
oranges." The sun is hot in my face, sweat does a number on my
eyes. "A revival, huh? She always was into Bible study an' all
that choir stuff. Even when she was in school she would carry a
Bible round wit her. Well, can I leave these wit you?"

"Yeah, come on in." He wiped his feet on the welcome mat.
He tailed behind me to the kitchen. I hoped he wasn't looking
at my ass. "You can sit 'em up there." I pointed to the porcelain
countertop.

"Can I trouble yuh fo' a drinka wata?"

I took a yellow pitcher from the refrigerator and poured the
water into one of Mama's glasses, the ones with the pink flowers.

"You want ice?"

"Naw, this is fine." He swallowed it down without as much
as a pause between gulps. Looked over my shoulder and noticed I had left my porn movies on the sofa. Always been careful

about leaving them out, so Ma wouldn't find them. It was no easy task.

"Tell me more 'bout how Ma was in school."

"She laughed 'bout everythang."

I took the videos and put them up on the highest shelf I could find.

"Whatchu puttin' up there?" He pulled the videos down.

"Nothin'. I was jus' fixin' up befo' Ma comes home." I watched nervously as he looked at the cover. He smiled.

"Oh, m'kay," he said, putting them back between the player and the chrome candleholders. There was nothing I could have done, no excuse I could come up with. Scared he would tell Mama about my porn. She thinks everything under the sun is a sin.

He slid one of the videos from between the chrome holders. *"Doing Danny.* Let's watch this one."

He slipped it into the player and pressed play. He sat down in the recliner next to me. Watched past the FBI warning, the promos of porn to come. It opened with two bears showering in a beach-house bathroom, kissing. I had only seen this one six or so dozen times. Brawny, soap-streaked men sucking nipples, groping heavy dicks with cock rings around tender balls. The credits rolled with fake, porn-star names. Darren Summers, Trent Rothschild. They started to blow each other. Lips. Suck. Slurp. Shower water bounced off their beefcake chests. I glanced over his crotch. His dick was hot against an inner thigh.

"Where you git these from?" he asked.

"Um 'pose to write a review on 'em for an online magazine. The editor sent 'em tuh me."

Sounded like he didn't believe me, but I didn't care. He started touching himself; my eyes were glued down below. He never looked off from the TV. He watched Darren Summers get his butt spit on and licked and split. I sank into the leather with legs spread. My left foot grazed a scuffed, dusty boot. I touched myself like the song, running my thumb across my dick. He looked at me as I looked at him. I let him watch what I was doing. He moved in closer, reaching over to touch me. I love another man's hand there. His was delicate. Not like other men that can be rough and meaningless.

His mouth was on it before too long. Head between my thighs, tongue in my middle. I looked down at mustache lips around cock muscle.

"Your tongue feels good." I pivoted myself into his mouth. Calloused fingers played with nipples as soft as a girl's. He knew just what to do. "Pinch 'em hard."

Sweaty ass. I look to the crucifix, Ma's pink Bible on the table, one of many in the house. It didn't take long to shoot white fire. He spit me into a glass of little pink flowers. Took a tissue from the table and cleaned. I looked at the clock that said a quarter till two.

"You got tuh go. She gon' be here in a few minutes." I stopped the movie we were watching and put it back in its case.

"Can we git togetha again?"

He pushed his dick back into his underwear. I damn near pushed him out the door. I needed to take a shower, didn't want Ma to catch him here.

"I'll call ya' tomorra." I had no intentions of doing this again, but I couldn't get him out of my head. The thought of him sucking.

I didn't think of him again till I came across his number on my dresser. Wish I had never laid eyes on it. It wasn't like I had a little black book. Men only like me 'cause I give good head. Dialed his number. Ringing and ringing. I was about to hang up when he picked up on his end.

"Hello?" I couldn't say anything. The words just wouldn't come out. "Hello? Hello?"

I hung up, only for the phone to ring again within minutes. Damn caller ID. I let it ring twice before I answered. Held the phone to my ear and said nothing. He said my name.

"Sorry 'bout that. Thought I had th' wrong numba."

"So wassup?" His voice was scratchy through the receiver.

"Nuttin'. Jus' thought I would see wassup witchu."

"So you only call me when you ain't got nuttin' to do, huh?"

I lied, told him I lost his number. It wouldn't have mattered. I had memorized it. Way he just tore into that melon, the juice running down his fingers that day at the flea market, dripping from his knuckles, made my dick hard. I wanted him to devour me like that, make my juices run.

"Can yuh bite intuh me like yuh bite intuh dat watamelon?"

"Whatchu say?"

"Nothin'. Neva min. Got plans t'night?"

"No. I was jus' 'bout tuh make some popcone an' watch th' game. But I ain't busy."

"Well, why 'on't I come ova an' we can find somethin' to do." I told him I would be there in half an hour. Ma was dead to the world with the TV on Soap Net. She can sleep through a hurricane. I was free-balling under the sweats tonight. I took the keys off the dining room table and snuck out quietly. I put the car in NEUTRAL and pushed it far enough up the dirt road. Neighbor's mutt barked. I got it up to Mrs. Emma's house. I jumped in and started the engine. "Made it."

Clouds of dew caked the windshield. The wipers wouldn't work. I left the window open. I looked at the address written on torn paper. *1132 Levy.* Drove down the street, read off the

numbers. *1122, 1129, 1132.* He lived in the same house as
Bruce, my daddy's friend, used to. Bruce was out mowing the
lawn when he keeled over with a heart attack. The house was
a different color from the dull brown it was then. Gray this
time, with white shutters. There was an engine in the carport, a
broken-down old Chevy Nova in the grass with four flat tires
and a popped hood exposing rusty no-good guts underneath.
The neighborhood was quiet, only the sound of cars trundling
past. I could see and hear the black-and-white TV from his living room. I checked my breath and rang the doorbell. I watched
through his window. I saw him and felt nauseous, nervous. I get
that way right before I'm about to fuck.

Beams of light seeped through the screen door.

"Come on in."

The house smelled like motor oil and fish sticks. Tools,
clothes and newspapers were strewn about. The TV was an old
floor model. The kind they don't make anymore. He must have
got it from some garage sale, the flea market. He's forever dragging something from out there. Somebody else's trash.

"Sorry 'bout the mess. Let me move soma' dis stuff out th'
way." Sofa springs squeaked when I sat down.

"Didjuh have problems findin' the place?"

"Naw, um pretty familiar wit this area."

"You want some to drank? I got beer, juice, Kool-Aid."

"I'll take a beer." He was dressed in a white tee and sweats,
a switch from the sun-bleached jeans. The sweats showed off his
booty nicely as they rode up the crack of his ass. Perfect with no
underwear.

Easy access. My dick was hot against me. I pulled and tugged
to keep it down. He came back with two cold beers.

"Jus' put th' popcone in th' microwave. It'll be ready in a
minute."

"You ain't got no watamelon in there?"

"Naw. Why?"

"Me an' Ma call you th' Watermelon Man."

"Why?"

"Every time we see you, you eatin' a slice."

His raspy burst of laughter erupted from deep depths. "I love it. Grew up on th' stuff."

"So who playin'?" I took a sip from my beer.

"Orlando Heat and the Blazers," he replied. "Fourteen-ten, Heat."

I really wasn't interested. I cocked my arm on the head of the smelly sofa. He was glued to the game, shouting. Going on like he was right there in the stadium making all that fuss. A piercing siren of sound came from the kitchen.

"Popcone's ready."

He left during a commercial. I watched from the living room as he poured the snack into a bowl. Every corner was packed with old furniture. Checked out his butt. My dick couldn't get any harder than it was already. Returned with the bowl of corn, shoving a handful in his mouth.

"Where you git all dis stuff from?"

"Flea market mos'ly, garage sales, Dumpstas. Lot of it's good stuff."

That explained the smell. I sat the bowl between us, aware of the mound in his sweats. My crazy dick was nowhere near what he had.

"I guess it beats them pricey furniture stores."

"Yep. Ain't nobody got dat kinda money."

I had my fill and moved the bowl to the coffee table.

"Yoon won't no mo'?"

"Naw, u'm full." I moved in closer to him. He smelled like deodorant soap. I slid my hands between and pulled. I took his dick. He didn't make a move. I yanked at elastic. Dick was bigger than most I've seen. It curled up to his stomach. I played with his tender foreskin. "Can I do it?"

"Go 'head."

I moved in and worshipped the most sensitive part. I looked into his eyes while I blew him. My hand was around his shaft with lips tight. A thick scent of crotch stink. Ma's childhood friend pushed me down on his dick.

"Open yo' mouth. Deep-throat it."

I gagged, but he didn't care. I got scared thinking about how he is when he's fucking. I went in deep. I didn't care what was on that old prehistoric TV. Pulled sweats around his ass. I wanted to see it all. I yanked them from his ankles and flung them who knows where. That nest of pubic hair. His dick in my mouth, cut-offs down and around. He reached over below, feeling me up. Them rough fingers between my booty.

"Stand up a minute. I wanna see that ass."

I turned around, giving him a grand view. He gave me a swift whack. It stung.

"Shake that ass."

I gave him a lap dance. He glided his dick along my ass. He grabbed and groped, leaned back into the sofa. Said, "Sit on it."

"Why don't I suck you off instead?"

"Wanna fuck you."

My ass is tighter than a maximum security prison. "Um real tight."

He jumped from the chair.

"I got some lotion." He fetched it from the bathroom. I finished getting undressed. Even tho he coulda took his time. I wasn't in a hurry to get fucked. The thought of it going in. What if he rips something? I reluctantly assumed the position. His greasy dick, a rush of the chills. Got it good and ready. He put some of the lotion in me.

"You gon' hafta go slow."

"I will."

I trusted him. It was a disaster with the last guy that tried. After hours he ended up falling asleep. I got away with my cherry attached.

I watched him from the mirror, behind the sofa, massaging his dick.

"Jus' relax." He held on to my hips.

That's what they all say. He started with a finger, loosened me up. I closed my eyes. Oh, the anticipation. He spread me with ease. Things went well. I felt the head of it. Hard, slow, take it easy. The pain bit me. Looked in the mirror and grimaced.

"You all right?"

"Jus' go slow."

The pain was less and less. Harder than a beer bottle, softer than a snack cake. He held on to my shoulders. Big bull dick. I watched him in the mirror. His pubes were rough across my ass. I gritted my teeth as he used me. The sweat poured. Mama would have had a heart attack if she saw me now. There was a string of semen. I was coming close. "Don't come in me."

His fingers sank into the flesh of my hips. Things were a blur. The house reeked of ass and popcorn. I grunted like a hog in heat. He pulled out. Shot it on me. Dismissed himself to the kitchen. He ran a dish towel over water. Wiped himself clean before returning. My belly was clean of come. I got dressed. Leg one, leg two into my sweats. I worked the neck of my tee over my head.

"Jus' rememba, I hafta call you, you cain't call me," I said.

He walked me to the door. I drove home with a sore ass. An anal virgin no more.

READY TO RIDE

Duane Williams

M y buddy Larry, who owns the farm next to mine, asked
if I might be looking for an extra hand for the summer.
"My nephew Jason from Toronto is gonna be spendin' July and
August with me and the wife," Larry explained. "He isn't gettin'
along too good with his parents apparently." I didn't ask any
questions and, to be honest, I wasn't keen about the idea. Larry
could see I was hesitating. "He's a real good kid, Neil. Says he
wants to be a farmer someday. Like his uncle, I guess." Larry
was charming me with his smile.

"Why doesn't he work for you then?"

"I can use him once the corn comes up, but that's not till
August. Besides, I already got my hired men for the season. You
won't be sorry if you take him on, Neil. I guarantee it."

Jason dropped by the next morning, after breakfast, to introduce himself. At eight in the morning, it was already another
sweltering day. I was lounging on the back porch in my boxers
with a coffee, watching Jason come up the lane on a bike. He

was shirtless. As he got closer, I could see that hiring him might be a good idea after all.

"Hi there. You must be Larry's nephew."

"Yeah. Hi. My name's Jason. And I bet you're Neil." Jason shook my hand with a vigorous grip. He said he was nineteen, although he looked older. He was definitely a looker. Thick, well-built shoulders for a kid. His pale, muscular arms were roped with veins. We stood on the back porch for a while, shooting the breeze about how the heat wave was taking its toll on farmers across the county.

"How do the cows do in this heat?" Jason asked. He seemed genuinely interested.

"Not great. They spend most of the day over there in the shade." I pointed at the cows in the pasture. "Yesterday, I had to cool them down with the hose. That or I would've had a shit load of steak on my hands."

Jason laughed as if on cue. "I love being out here in the country," he said. He took a deep breath in and held it for a moment in his barrel chest. "The air is so clean."

"Your uncle tells me you want to be a farmer."

"Yeah, and I've always wanted to be a vet too. I love animals. Especially horses. I think living on a farm is in my blood somehow."

"You take after your uncle, I guess."

"Yeah, my dad's always saying I should have been Uncle Larry's son." Jason rolled his eyes. "Ever since I visited an experimental farm in grade nine biology, I've wanted to be a vet or a farmer. My father thinks I should be a people doctor instead. But then again, he wants me to be lots of things I'm not." Jason had a hundred questions for me about farming and dairy cows. He wondered why I was living on the farm by myself. He was leading up to the question and finally asked, "Are you married?"

"No. I'm single and happy that way." I looked at him and winked. I didn't bother telling Jason I was divorced. Or a closet case, for that matter. Didn't make any difference really. Besides, I wanted to avoid the subject of Jennie. There were already too many rumors flying around the county about why we'd broken up.

"What about you? You got a girlfriend in Toronto?"

"No. Not really. Not right now anyhow."

I gave him a brotherly slap on the back. "Single life's more fun, buddy. Single guys get to fuck all they want. Nobody to answer to but your cock." Jason was smiling and nodding in agreement. "Looks like you work out," I remarked, squeezing his meaty shoulder.

"Yeah, I've been working out for a few years now," Jason said modestly. His chest alone deserved a blue ribbon—the light blond hair on his beefy pecs, his swollen, pink nipples, the kind you could chew on until morning. I shifted the growing bone in my boxers.

"Well, you look great. You're built like a farm boy."

Jason was blushing. "You think so?" He swatted away a horsefly as it dive-bombed his head.

"Definitely. How much can you bench?"

"Two forty-five's my best ever." The fly was buzzing around Jason's body, refusing to go away. "But I haven't been to the gym since my dad kicked me out last month." When the fly landed, it was near Jason's nipple. "So I've lost a little size, I think."

"Well, you look pretty damned good."

"Ouch!" With a sudden reflex, Jason flicked the fly off his chest. "Fuck. That hurt."

"Horseflies," I said. "They bite worse than me."

Jason looked down at the bite mark on his chest. "Look at that. The fucker drew blood."

"At least I don't draw blood. Not if you put a stake through my heart, that is." Jason squinted; he wasn't exactly sure how to take me. I could have jumped him right then and there. "When would you be ready to start?"

"Anytime you want me."

Truth was, I'd decided to give Jason a job the minute I saw him coming up the lane. "Farmwork's pretty tough. Sure you're up for it?" Jason nodded and smiled with excitement. "Only pays ten bucks an hour."

"That's great," he said, his blue eyes filled with enthusiastic fire. He was getting hotter every minute.

"Okay, you're hired." My dick pushed hard against the fly in my boxers. I reached down and gave it an obvious squeeze. Jason looked away, staring over where the cows were huddling in the shade.

"You think you'll have to hose them down again today?"

"If it gets any hotter, I will for sure."

"What time should I be here tomorrow?"

We made a quick plan for the next morning and said good-bye. Jason jumped on the bike, which was far too small for him, and rode fast down the lane, standing up on the pedals all the way to the road. His beautiful ass held high in the air. My new hired man.

The next morning Jason arrived at six, just like I had told him to. He looked half asleep. His blond curls were flat from a rest-less night in bed. "I hardly slept. Guess I was a little nervous about starting my new job," Jason said. I had to loan him a pair of my work boots because he was wearing running shoes.

Jason had never milked a cow, so I had to show him the ropes. He took to it like he'd been raised on a farm. He had no problem handling the cows, including shoveling up the shit.

He was even stronger than I'd expected, pushing around the bulls like they were harmless and weighed nothing. Within a few hours, Jason's T-shirt was soaked. As he peeled it off, I caught a whiff in the dusty air inside the barn. Jason was perfectly ripe.

And he was a hard worker, not lazy or complaining like some of the other boys I've had working for me. He did everything exactly as he was told and hardly spoke a word all morning. Didn't complain once about the heat in the barn, which, even for me, was stifling. I worked close by, mind you, to make sure Jason was doing things right. Whenever he squatted to plug the milkers on a cow, his crack peeked out over the top of his jeans, wooly and wet, soaking a line through his work pants.

While Jason was working on Daisy Beth, he asked me to come over and check out her teats. "They seem to be bleeding," Jason said. I went over and squatted beside him. I leaned into him until our shoulders touched, pretending to need a better look.

"Yeah, she's bleeding, all right," I said. "Happens a lot from these damned machines." I had the bag balm in my coveralls. As I spread the ointment on the cow's teats, Jason was standing beside me, his ass within striking distance. It took God-given strength not to drop the balm and go to work on that ass instead.

"Shit man, you're really sweating," I said as I finished up on Daisy Beth's teats. "Am I working you too hard?"

Jason shook his head. "Fuck no. I'm good." He caught a bead of sweat as it trickled from his furry armpit.

"Let's take a break. It's almost lunchtime anyhow."

We went to my office at the back of the barn, where I take care of the business end of running the farm. I cleared the papers off an old armchair and gestured for Jason to take a seat. "Don't mind the mess," I said. "The fan only half works and it's louder than hell, so I won't bother turning it on." I had two ice-cold beers in the fridge. "This should cool us down a bit."

We sat there sweating, chugging the beers, neither one of us saying a word. The long muscles in Jason's throat pulsated as he swallowed. Humidity and sexual tension were thick in the air. "I don't know about you," I finally said, "but I definitely need to get out of these sweaty clothes. I'm soaked, man." I went over and shut the office door. I stripped down to my boxers and sat down again with my beer. Jason looked a little surprised. He hesitated for a minute, playing with his beer can, turning it around in his hand, before he reached down and unbuttoned his pants. He wasn't wearing underwear, and his dick was already on the swell. It flopped out of his fly like a big bull's cock. He stepped out of his pants and stood there for a minute, making a show of his body, and I was the happy audience.

"Nice dick." Jason was thick and uncut. He looked down at his cock and gave it a tug. "Turn around so I can see your ass."

Jason grinned, then turned around without saying anything. He stood there with his hands on his hips. Jason had a small four-leaf clover tattooed on his butt, his asscheeks covered in the same fine hair as his chest. His ass was packed full of muscle. The hair caught the sunlight that was streaming in through cracks in the barn wall. I stopped cranking my dick, too close to unloading in my boxers.

"You ever done this before?" I asked, standing up behind him now.

Jason shook his head. "Just once when I was drunk." I nudged him on the back and he leaned forward against the bar fridge. He reached behind and opened his ass so I could get a good look at his sweet, wet hole.

"Fucking beautiful ass, man."

I dove right in with my tongue. It'd been a year since I tasted ass, and Jason's was worth the wait: raunchy and delicious. Jason was pushing back into my face, moving his hips around like his ass was on fire.

"Oh...that feels awesome," he said. I reached through his legs and squeezed his tight, loaded balls.

I was a hungry man, and Jason was groaning like he was about to split in two as I ate his hole. The kid could make a lot of noise. Out in the barn, one of the cows in heat was bawling up a storm. It was like she was calling back to Jason, who was equally horny and bothered. I pulled apart his cheeks and started fingering his tight, pink ring, circling it with my thumb. Jason was burning up, sweat rolling down his spine and into the crack of his ass.

"Try going inside," he said quietly like somebody besides me might hear. After juicing up his hole with a spitball, I tried one finger, then two. On two, he gasped and arched his back. "That hurts a little," he said. I grabbed the dusty tube of Vaseline out of my desk, and I tried again. Soon he was begging for three fingers. "Oh shit, yeah...that feels great. Go a little deeper."

Jason was ready to ride now, his body shuddering as I opened his meaty hole with my fingers. My dick bobbed in anticipation. I put in a fourth finger and Jason started begging to get plowed. He reached back and grabbed my dick, guiding it raw into his hole. Between him and the cow, I almost didn't hear the truck coming up the lane. I wasn't inside him ten seconds before Jason blew his whole load of cream on the office floor.

When Larry came into the office, Jason and I were dressed again. I'd thrown some old newspapers over Jason's puddle of jizz on the floor. Jason was sitting in the musty armchair in his pants and no shirt, flushed, finishing his beer.

"Just dropped by to see how you boys are makin' out," Larry

said, looking at me suspiciously. Jizz lingered in the air. "Quite a hot one for your first day Jason."

"Yeah, it gets really frigging hot in the barn. It's hard work, but I'm liking it so far."

"He's doing a great job, Larry."

Larry looked at me. "No complaints?"

"None yet." I smiled at him.

Larry hung around in the office for a few minutes, looking around at things as we stood there, awkwardly shooting the breeze. Then he went on his way into town. As his pickup was going down the lane, Jason and I were already back to doing chores. The kid didn't say a word for the rest of the day. He was serious and worked even harder than he did in the morning, the ass of his pants soaked through. When the milking was done and the cows were back in pasture, I showed him cleanup procedures, and we called it a day.

"You did a great job today," I said, giving him a jock slap on the butt. "Coming back tomorrow?"

"For sure," he said, smiling at me. "If that's okay?"

"We got lots more to do around here," I said. "I'll see you at six sharp."

Jason jumped on his bike, and I watched that unforgettable ass as he rode like hell down the lane, throwing a trail of dust behind him. When he reached the road, Jason looked back at me and waved. Tomorrow's forecast was for an even hotter day in the county.

WELL WISHING

Steve Berman

The salesman tasted the dust in the air streaming through the open windows as he drove down the dirt road. The Ford Fairlane's faulty air-conditioning, wheezing, failed to chill the interior against a blinding August sun. The right front tire popped suddenly. The car shuddered, especially the steering wheel. The salesman cursed as he guided the sedan to the side of the road.

Outside, he bent down on ailing knees to look at the flat tire. His bright red tie hung like a panting dog's tongue in the heat of the late day. He cursed more on his way to the trunk. There had to be a spare somewhere underneath the sample boxes. But he couldn't find one.

He remembered passing a farmhouse. They'd have a phone, though he'd rather have a faucet to splash cold water over his head. He took his briefcase and suit jacket, out of habit. He didn't bother locking the car; if someone wanted to come along and take the plumbing supply brochures and sales charts, he was welcome to do so. Few clients had this season. He rolled up the sleeves of his damp dress shirt and began walking.

There once was a lonely farmer's son who visited the heads of
his lovers in an old wishing well.

The salesman knocked on the farmhouse door. The wooden
boards of the porch creaked underneath his feet. A gruff and
grim face peered out when the door opened slightly.

"You look like a feller that sells somethin'." The man looked
ready to spit from tobacco-stained lips.

"No, wait." The salesman reached out and the palm of his
hand smacked against the closing door. "My car broke down a
mile from here. I just want to use your phone."

A softer, gentler voice spoke from somewhere behind the man.
"Pa, let the poor man in." Thick fingers with brightly painted
nails reached around and pulled the door aside.

The salesman offered his Closing Grin, the most sincere
expression in his limited repertoire. The frowning old man remained blocking the threshold. A young girl beside him, shorter
and stouter but very pretty with long blonde hair, took hold of
one of the farmer's overall straps and pulled him back.

"Forgive Pa. He likes them canvassers 'bout as much as he
does Eisenhower." She reached out and took the salesman's arm.
Her strong grip guided him into a parlor. Dust motes danced in
the shreds of sunlight from open windows.

"I'll bring you a glass of iced lemonade." She pushed him
down onto the tufted sofa. His rump felt an inch or so of pad-
ding before reaching the hard wood backing. He immediately
missed the sedan's front seat, which felt like an opulent throne
in comparison.

The old man leaned into the parlor's doorway. "Kids are
trustin'. Too trustin' for my likin'. What's wrong with the car?"

"Flat tire."

"George can tow ya into town. Has a plum garage."

The girl returned with a sweating glass. She leaned down farther than necessary, offering a view of her bosom. The salesman
made sure to reach for the glass with his left hand, mindful to
show off the gold wedding ring. The girl took notice and her lips
puckered. After the salesman took a sip his did too. He managed
to force a slight smile. "The phone?" Half his voice seemed lost
after swallowing.

"In the kitchen," said the farmer.

"Stay for dinner," said the daughter.

They led the salesman to where a black Bakelite beast hung
on the wall. It looked like the misbegotten child of the iron stove
across the room.

*Whenever he could, the farmer's son would sneak out of the
house or away from his chores and go to the well. He had found
it years ago, overgrown and empty, the faded Wishing Well sign
on the ground. Three heads bobbed in the dark water now. He
knew them well. The first belonged to the neighbor's boy. It was
the favorite of the farmer's son, who would often comb the wet
curly hair away from blue eyes. The second had been an accident. He shouldn't have been drinking with his sister Claire's
beau that night. The third and most recent head had such heavy
jowls often only the thick lips and dimpled chin would surface
and gulp air. The local Justice of the Peace, now just pieces.*

The mechanic annoyed the salesman, but conveyed the sense
that yes, he would tow the car and yes, he would change the
tire, and for an extra fee and some extra time, could fix the air-
conditioning.

That meant the salesman would have to find someplace to

spend the night. He opened his wallet to the farmer. He had no idea if the farmer even knew who Andrew Jackson was. "I could sleep on your sofa if you don't have a spare bed." Though he instantly regretted the idea. The floorboards or the dirt outside might be softer. Out of the corner of his eye, the salesman caught a glimpse of the daughter twirling a lock of hair around her fingers.

The back screen door opened and a short young man walked into the kitchen. The rivulets of sweat that ran down his forehead and neck streaked dirty skin. A few tufts of dried grass clung to close-cropped hair. Like the old farmer, he wore overalls, but nothing else.

He snatched the glass of lemonade the salesman had set down. He drained it in one long drink. Drops of condensation fell onto the top of his chest, mixing with the sweat to reveal tanned skin under caked dust.

The salesman found himself staring. Habit made him twist the warm gold ring around and around on his finger.

"My boy," said the farmer with a grunt.

"Dan." The young man had curving wet lips. "You sellin' somethin'?"

"No." The salesman found his mouth dry. He regretted not getting more of the sour lemonade. "Just had a bit of car trouble."

"Trouble happens a lot around here." Dan wiped his forehead clear with the glass.

His sister punched him in the arm. "No need to be rude."

The farmer snatched the twenty-dollar bill from the salesman's hand. "We got an extra room. Belonged to Gran before she passed. You can sleep there."

Without another word, Dan returned to the outdoors, which made sense to the salesman; the young man looked like a wild thing. The girl began to putter about the kitchen, taking down pots and pans, reaching into the humming refrigerator. She gave the salesman a wink when she bent over to add wood to the stove.

The salesman followed after the farmer, up creaking stairs and down a dark hallway to the last room. It looked like no one had been inside in decades. The salesman sneezed twice at the smell of must and age. A faded quilt covered the bed.

"Even though I took your money, know I'll be listenin'. Beds squeak in this house," said the farmer.

"Sorry?"

"I mean to have my daughter Claire married to the right man, not some slick. You even think of payin' her a midnight visit and I'll introduce you to the other members of the house. Holland and Holland."

The salesman laid a hand on the bed. The rise of disturbed dust was accompanied by a cry of protest from the springs. "That would be a gun, I take it?"

The farmer nodded. "My beloved. Spits better than me." But the man still hawked his throat clear to land a brownish gob near the salesman's loafers.

The farmer's son knew that the heads in the well were his only friends. He would slip through the thick brush that surrounded the well and sit next to the cool stone walls, one hand draped over the side so his fingers could splash the water. He would call out to the heads and they would rise to the surface. The first, his first love too, came quickest, rising like a pink champagne bubble. Then his sister's boyfriend, and finally, after many taps on the surface, Justice. As he talked, they would smack their lips, reminding him of hungry pet goldfish he had won as a child one county fair. Those had died real quick, but not the heads.

Sometimes, if the son leaned in far enough and brought his ear close to them, he could hear them weakly speak his name and ask for favors. Mostly the heads wanted company.

After thirty years selling plumbing supplies throughout the Midwest, the salesman knew his way around bathrooms. The same bad jokes at the annual sales conference in Chicago: beefsteaks, cigars, and the stalls at Union Station men's room.

He recognized the claw-foot at the farmhouse as a Lang Slipper, model A. In 1941, the tub would have gleamed with fresh, white porcelain over wood; now it looked as dingy as he felt. He turned the faucets. The water spilling out stayed a murky brown while he counted past ten, but remained hot. He tempered it with a splash from the cold water tap.

He stripped off his clothes, leaving his ring and watch on top of the commode. He sat in the tub as it filled, balancing soap on his wide, hairy stomach. The water that rose around the bar became cloudy and the smell of lemongrass reached his nose.

The salesman slipped further down into the tub and dunked his head underneath the water, only for a few seconds that left the world warm and silent but for the slight whoosh of his hands moving through the bath. But when he came up and blinked away the sudsy water, the salesman saw the farmer's son sitting on the edge of the tub. One overall strap hung undone, exposing a portion of bare chest. The salesman would have been startled but for Dan's smile.

The young man looked freshly scrubbed, skin almost as golden as his hair from the sun. "Where have you been?"

The salesman didn't know exactly what answer the young man sought. He shrugged. "Both coasts and lots of nowhere in between."

"I've never left the farm."

The salesman let his wet hand rise to the tub edge not far from Dan's leg. One finger had a tan line.

"Always alone?" Dan held up the wedding band between his thumb and forefinger. The ring looked flimsy.

The salesman nodded. "A trick. The world caters to married men." He slid his hand along the porcelain glaze onto Dan's thigh. "But I'm not the marrying kind."

Dan nodded. "I know some tricks." He opened his mouth wide while leaning his head back. Then he dropped the gold ring in.

"Suppose that was a family heirloom." The salesman smirked, remembering how he had found the ring many years ago in a demo sink's P-trap. His first sales call. The client had laughed and wondered if Link & Grant Plumbing Supplies offered prizes, like the treat inside a Cracker Jack box, with every purchase.

"You can try and get it back." Dan half leaned in, half slid down, his mouth open to show the ring that glittered like a lure on the back of his tongue. The salesman reached out with dripping arms and pulled Dan into the tub. Their faces pressed hard, mouths forceful. The salesman's tongue sought the ring almost as an afterthought of exploring new territory.

"Haven't found it yet," laughed Dan. He splashed more water about while squatting over the salesman and unbuckling the remaining denim strap. His torso had been kissed by sun and youth and now water, which made the skin gleam like bronze fixtures.

"Shhh," the sound slid out of the salesman like steam. "Your father—"

"Is in bed with the Hollands after visitin' Jim Beam awhile in the kitchen. He wants you to stay away from my sister. I do too."

"I promise," said the salesman, who pressed his mouth back to the young man's chest. He heard Dan moan slightly and mutter, "It's best for all of us."

The farmer's son leaned over the well's edge to dip his fingertips in the cool water. Now and then one of the heads would idly bump against his hand. He noticed that the water's surface dimpled, before realizing tears fell from his face. He wiped his cheeks. The heads in the well were not enough. They could barely whisper. If lifted from the well, they'd become listless. The farmer's son wanted to hear a man, whether his own name grunted or gently said. He missed the feel of hands upon his body and of touching warm skin, tracing fingers through sweat.

But the farmer's son could not escape. Not from the farm, with its daylight of endless chores and nighttime of quiet need. Not from the well, for fear that the heads would sink to the bottom and rest there like stones cast away. The land belonged to the family for generations and owned him. His loneliness kept him at the well as much as it had brought the heads to the water.

The next day, the salesman sat on the rickety porch. Yesterday's hateful sun had been traded for a milder sibling. He fingered the jacket across his lap, the briefcase close at hand, the warm ring on his finger. He had reclaimed it from Dan only after the water had cooled and puddled on the floorboards.

The salesman had found the mattress lumpy and lonely. He had wanted to slip with Dan under the muslin sheets and fall asleep together, but Dan had given him a sad look while blotting the spilled water from the tub.

The familiar sound of his sedan came down the road. He stood up, feeling the years in his lower back and knees. He turned back to the farmhouse, but the only face in the window belonged to the girl.

On the walk between bathroom and bedroom last night, the salesman had passed an open door. By the weak light from the room's window, he had glimpsed the farmer's daughter sitting up in bed, one hand toying with the strings at the front of her nightgown.

The salesman had rested a hand on the doorknob. She lifted and pulled one string taut revealing more of her chest. He shut her door.

The salesman promised himself to schedule another visit soon on the same route. Perhaps before summer's end. He glanced around at the surrounding fields and raised a hand in farewell for Dan, wherever he might be.

The farmer's son wondered often if the rest of the world might be as magical as the well. Or had he found the only such spot on earth. Both ideas scared him.

The Home Office felt like anything but home. Too many desks filled with secretaries typing, chatting, and trying to catch everyone's eye. Too many rooms filled by other salesmen boasting, laughing, and trying to surpass the next guy's numbers. Water coolers gurgled.

The salesman sat by the far end of the conference room table. During his years with Link & Grant, he had moved closer to where the CEO sat, before plunging back down to the bottom to sit beside some wiry rookie who sweated over Delaware's routes.

The salesman rubbed at his temples, wishing away the terrible headache that had begun after lunch. Along with a few of the other old-timers, he had gone to a steakhouse and shared cuts of red beef and tumblers of amber whiskey.

His hand shook when he dropped a cube of pure white sugar into his cup. He watched it bob up and down in the miniature black sea as the CEO droned on and on about the price of copper. The immersed cube remained sharp-edged, stained but intact. With a tiny spoon, the salesman stabbed at the sugar, but it refused to dissolve. When he took a sip, he crushed it between his teeth. The taste made him feel worse.

His throat began to ache and he loosened his tie.

Minutes later, he disrupted the meeting by rising and leaving the room quickly with a muttered excuse.

Every employee had a key to the bathroom, a showcase for the company. Each sink and faucet and toilet was different from the next: rows of gleaming brass and stainless steel and old bronze over porcelain bowls.

Out of habit, the salesman went to the farthest, which featured a gilded tap shaped like a swan's neck. He turned the spigot to create a strong flow. His reflection looked pale, his eyes watery.

He splashed cold water onto his face, his neck. He drank from cupped hands. The wet ring on his finger glittered.

When he looked up at the mirror, he saw he was not alone in the bathroom. It took him a moment to recognize the farmer's daughter standing in the shadows of the stalls.

"You're like all the others. Come a callin' but never pay me no mind."

The salesman turned around. He stared at the row of empty toilets. He spun back and in the mirror she stood behind him. Her reflection clutched the back of his neck; he could feel icy hands thrust his head down into the sink's basin.

The salesman closed his eyes to the water, so cold it numbed the pain of striking the porcelain. She shoved his face through

the slender drain, the pressure of the pipes mashing his cheek-
bones, his chin. Then he broke loose at the neck, felt buoyant
and relieved, and the stream of water carried him off.

*The farmer's son came to the well that afternoon and saw the
shiny ring sitting atop the crumbling mortar. He knew before
even looking that his sister had added another head. He picked
up the ring and leaned over the side. The surface was dark; the
heads hid whenever she came by. Tearful, he called out to them,
cajoling each to rise up. The salesman's head with its gray hair
swirling in the water moved near and allowed him to pet it. The
farmer's son would have gladly traded the ring, the sun, anything to kiss a pair of lips a second time.*

THE FARMER'S SON

Karl Taggart

The motorcycle broke down without warning, just crapped out like the engine had been snuffed, so I coasted to the shoulder and thought, *What the hell?* I'd roared out of L.A. after a shitty week at work, heading north and cutting over to Highway 99 and the central valley because I wanted away from the monotony of I-5 and the familiarity of coastal 101. So that's how this city boy ended up stranded in farm country, far short of a motel in Visalia, the nearest burg. Fields surrounded me, rows of cabbage that had taken over when rows of onions ran out. I'd enjoyed riding along with the wind in my face, sucking in the various vegetable smells, the vastness of it all reminding me just how big California is and how easily we coastal city dwellers forget it's an agricultural state. But then the bike quit and everything changed.

I got off and looked at the thing. I knew enough to determine the engine wasn't getting any gas, which probably meant a clogged fuel line, so with the help of a tiny tool kit extracted from its hidey-hole under the seat, I managed to unhook the fuel lines and blow them out, none of which helped. The thing would not run. "Fuck," I said aloud, then again, and again, finally exploding into a string of profanity until a car honked its horn as it zoomed by and I realized I'd taken on the look of a madman. So I sat on the bike, trying to decide my next move.

Part of the upset was that I had, in my hasty exit, tossed aside my cell phone as some kind of statement that I needed no connection to anyone. Now I wondered if this reckless move hadn't created some awful karma. It was as I accepted my own contribution to the situation that I looked across the fields on the opposite side of the highway and saw a farmhouse in the distance. It was small and gray, and I wondered if it was even inhabited. But as dusk was fast upon me, I locked the bike and started walking. Soon I stepped onto a rickety porch and knocked at a door sorely in need of paint. A grizzled old man in overalls with a paper napkin tucked into the bib answered.

"Sorry to bother you," I began, "but I've broken down on the highway. Can I use your phone to call a tow?"

"Murphy's Garage," the man said, "'cept he'll be closed now. C'mon in, we can help you out, but supper's on."

The house had the cramped feel of a place built a couple centuries back, and the furniture looked that period, faded velvet sofa and chairs in an awful dark green. The family sat around an oval table in the dining room, two young men and one young woman.

"Fella broke down," the old man announced.

The others nodded and went back to their chicken, which smelled good and made me realize how hungry I was.

"That's Tom," the old man said, "and his wife June and over there's Billy, my other son who ain't got a wife. My name's Bob Stremple."

"Scott Raynes," I said. "I really appreciate this."

There was little talk beyond Bob telling me Billy was good with motors and might be able to fix my car.

"Actually, it's a motorcycle."

Bob nodded and Billy's mouth dropped open. He was big and blond, handsome in a bearish way. "What kind?" he asked.

"Triumph six-fifty. Ran fine until now."

He nodded, taking this in, then Bob said it was too late to fix it tonight so I should stay over. When supper was finished June cleared the dishes while we men went to watch TV. Around nine, when June had settled beside Tom and he'd begun to rub her thigh, they said goodnight and went down the hall. When they'd gone Bob reminded Billy there was much to do the next day and Billy rose and left us. Then Bob turned to me.

"You'll bunk in with Billy but I don't want no foolin' around, you hear? Billy gets up to things sometimes and I get after him about it so don't you go and let him fuck you."

The next second dissolved into a long, surreal moment in which I realized I'd stepped into a cliché, and, further, that it was going to play out. Maybe not the traditional way because that story was a farmer's daughter, but still, it was happening pretty much as written. And I wondered in the next long moment if maybe this wasn't even real, if maybe it was a dream and I was asleep in a motel in Visalia with my dick in my hand and the bike had never broken down at all. But I found myself nodding to Bob, unable to form words, and he stood and said, "I'll turn in too. Billy's room is second door down the hall, next to the bath."

I followed him into the hall and as his door closed behind him the bathroom door opened and out stepped darling Billy, stark naked. A jolt ran through me, radiating from my dick, while Billy just stood smiling as if nakedness in the family hallway was perfectly natural. He was over six feet tall, thick,

solid, and furred with more of the blond that curled so beauti-
fully on his head. Without a word he opened his bedroom door
and as I entered I noticed his hand on his dick almost absently,
as if that was also perfectly natural.

He was in proportion down there, big dick for a big man,
and as he hardened I noted the blond thicket where the cock
grew. Bob's words echoed in my head, "Don't you go and let
him fuck you," and I almost laughed at how futile the request
was. I began to undress.

As Billy pulled back the covers, I thought of him dutifully
making his bed each morning, which gave him a certain innocent appeal—farm boy schooled in the basics but little more. His
life centered on crops and animals and family; he was earthiness
incarnate, and when I stood bare before him, he grinned almost
shyly. His cock pointed at me now and he pulled on it slowly,
gently, as he eyed me up and down.

"I can fix your bike," he said, which surprised me.

"You have experience with motorcycles?"

"No but it's an engine and I'm good with 'em, keep everything on the farm running."

"It's not getting gas," I said as he approached.

"Carburetor, maybe, or a fuel line," he replied.

"No, I checked it all." He put a hand on my cock, thumbed
the tip.

"I'll figure it out," he said as he knelt and then I was in his
mouth and nothing on wheels mattered.

In seconds I was frantic, thrusting at him while he sucked me.
I ran my fingers into his wet curls and when I started to come
I held the yell to a muffled grunt, mindful of Bob's admonish-
ment.

It was an exquisite long climax, possibly because this gorgeous bear of a man was expertly pulling it out of me and also

because I hadn't been sucked or fucked in weeks, which was part of the reason I'd fled L.A. in the first place. Billy sucked until I ran dry and even then kept at me, playing with my soft morsel. Finally he let go, looked up and smiled. I thought about Bob as I climbed into bed.

Billy stood holding himself and eyeing me like he was deciding which piece to eat first. He even licked his lips. Then he crawled onto the bed and began to explore the whole of me with his big rough hands, finally turning me over and parting my buttcheeks, which caused him to suck in a long breath before getting down between my legs. As he held me open, I felt hot breath in my crack, then a tongue. Bob had every reason to worry.

I had never before been devoured so completely and as I shuddered with delight I wondered if country living had encouraged this big bear to simply do what came naturally, to feed his desires, literally, never mind the limits of society—or his father.

His tongue was a marvel, pushing in deeply then poking around like some snake in search of prey. Mouth plastered to me, Billy crawled around in my chute until he had me squirming and then, as if he hadn't done enough, he began a tongue-fuck unlike anything I'd ever known. As he went at me, a corner of my mind—the tiny part still able to form coherent thoughts— wondered where he'd learned all this, because it was too good to simply be something he'd fallen into. He was expert, beyond a doubt. What on earth went on out here in the middle of nowhere? But then he withdrew and sat back and I rolled over to look at him licking his lips with that tongue and then he was on me, pinning me in a full body press as he shoved his tongue into my mouth.

I passed a moment in which I considered that it had just been up my butt but this quickly faded as his tongue set up a dance with mine. He began to grind his big hard wet dick against my

belly while he kissed me hard and he kept on for several minutes, then pulled off, grinned, and said with a sort of childish
glee, "Let's fuck."

Turned out he was well prepared, and I discarded his innocence as mere illusion. He got off the bed, opened a dresser
drawer and took out several condoms, a tube of lube, a dildo
and a handful of other stuff that looked to be tangled with a
long string of anal beads. He suited up, greased himself, and
told me to get on my back. His commands had the ring of Bob
Stremple; I did as told.

He ran a gob of lube into me and I sucked in a breath as he
poked his big cock at my rim. His eyes were on mine, sparkling
now, I swear, his face flushed, his mouth open, tongue out like
it wanted to fuck again. And then he pushed in, not easily, not
with care but with the thrust of the animal he was and he set off
on a slamming stroke that set the bed creaking and I thought of
Bob across the hall and hoped he was a heavy sleeper.

I wanted to work my dick while Billy did me but couldn't
manage anything more than holding on because he had me in
his thrall and I was loving it. His face registered every bit of his
pleasure and I watched it go from wonder and passion to bear-
ing down and biting his lip at one point, then that tongue getting
loose, caught between lips locked into a grimace I knew all too
well. Grunting then, going at it full out, bed screeching under
the onslaught, then sudden silence from him, eyes closing as he
let go his load, pumping it into me for what seemed forever. I
pictured not the spurts of most men but great gushes and a condom stretched beyond capacity.

When he'd emptied and stopped, he didn't have the look of a
man who's finished but of a man just getting started. He grinned
as he pulled out, stripped the rubber and held it up like some
prize. The thing was heavy with spunk. "Be right back," he said

as he stood up and tossed the thing. "Gotta wash." And he was gone naked down the hall while I still lay with legs up, happily and thoroughly fucked.

When he came back minutes later his big dick was at rest, hanging heavily over a pair of fat balls. I noted, as he entered the room and closed the door, a change of demeanor, the ass-eating, butt-fucking bear now hesitant, almost shy, looking at me, then away, blushing. I saw he wanted something else.

"What is it, Billy?" I asked as I sat up. My cock was hard from the fuck and I had a hand on it, hoping he'd suck me off again—but he avoided me now because I'd seen something in him, something he maybe thought wrong, so I pressed further. "That was some fuck," I told him. "You're really good, Billy. You can do whatever you want to me."

He kept his head down, looking at me from under his brows, then worked himself up to spilling it. "I want you to do it to me," he said, then looked away.

"What? Fuck you?"

He nodded. "From behind," he said to the floor. "Like a bull does."

Holy shit, I thought, squeezing my drooling dick. "You ever been fucked?" I asked.

He shook his head. "Just the rubber one but I like it up there."

"Oh, Billy," was all I could say.

He was so different then, getting me a condom and lube, making sure all was in order before he climbed onto the bed and stuck his butt up. He was furred back there and his crack, where I'd soon have my dick, was a riot of blond. I got in behind him, applied the rubber and lube, then hesitated with a finger full for him. Billy, surprisingly perceptive, reached back and pulled open his buttcheeks to such an extent that his hole quivered before me. "Give me some grease," he said. "Lots."

I ran several gobs up him, mindful I rarely topped anyone though far from adverse to it. Caught up in the thrill of being taken, I'd almost forgotten the rewards of reciprocity so I found myself in an oddly grateful state of mind. This big bear of a man was giving me his all.

When he was awash in lube I eased my dick into him, listening to his little moans that accompanied my progress. When I was all the way in he squeezed me and held fast which impressed me but then he was muscular all over so why not there?

When I began to ride him he chuckled and when I had a good stroke going I slapped his ass, which got an "Oh yeah" out of him and I saw we were now cowboy and bronc, me in the saddle, him cutting loose below.

As I rode and slapped and held off yelling *yee-hah*, I tried to recall the last guy I'd done but found only an unsatisfying blur, which was to Billy's credit, darling Billy who was likely in the process of erasing much of my sexual memory.

When my juice began to rise, I couldn't help letting go verbally as well and I asked Billy if he liked taking dick up the ass, liked getting fucked, and he responded to each demand like some raging Baptist calling out *amen* to his pastor's holy exhortations. "Praise the dick," I said, in keeping with this thought and Billy responded, "Fuck me, lordy yes, fuck me," and there I was unloading into this big furry ass, this big furry man, and I saw the world anew, healed, righted, brilliant before me, untroubled and oh god, how good it is when you're coming.

I wore myself out on Billy, finally slumping onto him and sliding out, then collapsing as if about to expire. With what seemed my last breath I managed a raspy "Hallelujah" and Billy responded with another "Praise the dick."

We lay side by side after, Billy with hands across his chest, eyes closed, breath steady, and I thought of all kinds of things to say but said none. Instead I went to sleep.

He awakened me at dawn, greased, sheathed, and ready. "Shush," he said as his cock went in even though I'd made no sound. He lay on his side behind me, going at it, and as he fucked he reached over to get hold of me and started an equal motion so I was done front and back which caused me to dissolve into a sort of swoon, not sure I was even awake because isn't this every man's dream?

But soon he grunted, rammed it home, then worked me enough to make me shoot, after which he declared it time to get up and fix the bike. I found this dose of reality unwelcome as I was ready to stay naked with him and fuck away the rest of my life but he was out of bed and into overalls—without underwear, just a T-shirt—and I saw the last of his great cock.

In the early morning chill Billy looked over the motorcycle, which we'd rolled over from the highway, while I stood watching. He did much of what I already had—to no avail—then stood pondering for a bit. Finally he smiled, unscrewed the gas cap, poked a finger around both the outside and inside, and took out a pocket knife—but before he went to work he showed me my problem. "Airhole's plugged," he said and I looked at the pinhole in the cap, probably the most unnoticed thing on a motorcycle.

"Something's in there," Billy went on. "Dirt. Bug, maybe. No air comin' in, no gas goin' out." And he dug the point of his blade into it, extracted the ick, wiped it on his overalls, then put the cap back on. "Give her a try," he said.

"It can't be," I replied, laughing. But it was. The bike sputtered then started and with a few twists of the throttle began a familiar purr.

"I never would have thought of that," I said and Billy, standing with hands in his pockets, grinned and I thought how much

I liked this man, how almost foreign he seemed compared to my usual partners and how refreshing this was. I also thought of that big dick, free inside those baggy overalls, and I wondered if other men had come to call or would in the future. But then I saw Bob Stremple on the porch and Billy turned back into the boy. "Got her running, Pa."

Bob came down to us. "So I see. Breakfast is on."

"You hungry?" Billy asked and I said no, I'd best get on my way because I knew if I went back inside I'd never want to leave. I shut off the bike, went to Bob and shook his hand. "Thanks for putting me up and the supper last night. You saved a weary traveler and it is much appreciated."

He looked me over then and I wondered what he might have heard during the night and if he was leading up to calling me on it but he just let go of my hand and nodded. "You ever out this way again, you stop by."

Billy laughed at this and Bob passed him a look that made the boy clamp his mouth shut but he still grinned from ear to ear.

"Bye, Billy," I said as I got back on the bike. "Maybe I will ride up this way again."

He looked at me in that singular way a man does when he's had his dick up you and he nodded. When I started the engine he laughed and as I rode away I gave thanks to the bug or whatever it was that had crawled into that gas cap and given me the time of my life.

WRESTLING GATORS

Vincent Diamond

I don't remember which made my heart beat faster—the twelve-foot alligator sunning itself on the left bank of the pond or the naked, six-foot-plus blond guy asleep on the right.

The gator I was expecting—I'm a wildlife wrangler working the Tampa Bay region. What used to be swamp and pine forests has gotten bought up and turned into gated developments and jogging trails. Problem is, no one has found a way to tell the animals that they've been evicted. That was kinda my job.

The golf course called me in to catch this gator. It was big enough not to be intimidated by the golf carts *or* the golfers. A player had whacked at the gator with a club yesterday, and the reptile just hissed and snapped at the guy. The manager called me when the foursome got back to the clubhouse.

My Ford pickup was an early '80s model with real spark plugs, a carburetor, and an eight-cylinder engine I tuned to run in near-silence, a necessity when you chase wild animals for a living. It rumbled quietly beneath me as I let the truck idle closer to the pond. Somewhere in the woods a blue jay screeched and a nice May breeze ruffled the kid's hair.

The gator's eyes stayed closed. So did the blond kid's.

Now that I was closer, I could see that he was midtwenties, maybe. Maybe not really a kid, but young to me. I'd turned thirty-five in December and weird as it was, that got to me even more than turning thirty had. It's not like I was a doddering old man, but I sure noticed my hard days lately: chasing through the woods after a hog, or climbing through some old lady's attic for a possum. Wildlife wrangling isn't exactly like a desk job, you know? A lot of nights I got home; took a long, hot shower; jerked off, and was in bed—asleep—by nine o'clock. I'd even gotten a heating pad for my back.

Looking this guy over on a warm May morning made me heat up somewhere else, though. He was fair-skinned, not so white as to be sickly looking, just creamy skinned, with freckles on his lower arms and a few on his face. His chest was smooth, muscled. Not that fancy-boy look you get from weightlifting— more like he worked for a living, too. Golden fuzz started just below his belly button and turned into thick and springy pubic hair above his cock. It was cream-colored too, lying slender and soft against his pink testicles, so pale that I wondered if he'd put sunscreen on it. A real blond, this kid. The sun glinted in the highlights of his reddish-gold pubic hair. His long legs were slim and evenly muscled.

My cock snaked up in my shorts and began to pay attention.

I could have just watched him and jerked off in my truck but I wanted to give him a try. It was hokey but the Knight in Shining Armor routine might work here. I put the truck in PARK and grabbed the cattle prod from my gun rack.

When I got about four yards away from him, I spoke quietly. "Sir, wake up please, but don't move. Wake up!"

His eyelids twitched and one hand made a brushing away don't-bother-me jerk.

"Sir, wake up, please. This is urgent. Wake up, you could be in some trouble." I let my voice get harder, deeper.

"Huh? Wha?" The kid opened his eyes and they made me stop short. The palest blue-gray, his eyes looked alien, surreal. They stood out from his golden skin like pearls. His gaze locked on me, the truck, the cattle prod, and his whole body stiffened. Not in quite the way I'd imagined, but still. Reality never matches fantasy, ya know?

"Wake up and stay absolutely still." I nodded over to the gator.

He looked over, too. "Jesus Christ!"

"No, that's an alligator."

He scrabbled backward, his feet tangling in the beach towel, falling back on his elbows.

I bent down and offered a hand. "Don't move fast, just get up real quiet like and we'll get to the truck."

He grabbed my hand—hard—and we stood up. He wobbled a little, pressed against me to balance, and Mr. Rascal came to half attention in my shorts. He bent over to snag his clothes, showing me a muscled ass. Nice. We eased back toward my truck, me playing the Knight with that silly cattle prod pointing toward the gator. I opened the passenger door and he leaned against the seat. He didn't seem too worried about being naked in front of me. And I sure wasn't complaining. Now that I was up close, I saw there was a fine layer of grit and pond dirt on his skin, left over from his swim. He was taller than I was, maybe six-three, and I found myself counting the freckles on his chest. He was so different from the dark, hairy Italian that I saw in the mirror every morning.

He saw me looking and held out one hand. "Paul."

"Denny," I said as we shook hands. "You're not from around here, are you?"

"No, I'm down from Michigan, visiting my sister. She has a condo on the fourteenth fairway."

"Didn't she tell you not to go swimming in freshwater?"

"We didn't really get a chance to talk much. I got in late last night and she had to go to work this morning."

"Shoot, you're lucky that gator didn't want you for breakfast. I seen 'em snap through a turtle shell like we snap a crab claw."

"Jesus Christ," he said again. He pushed back his damp hair with trembling hands. I could practically see the adrenaline kicking through his system—adrenaline and fear. His face was flushed. "Was that thing in the water with me?"

I looked over at the gator; its skin glistened in the sunshine. "Yeah, it looks like he's been swimming."

"Fuck."

"Love to." I met his strange gaze, those pale eyes on me like moonlight.

He smiled. He ran one hand over my chest, fingers tweaking at my nipples. Before I knew it, his lips were against me, then his tongue, probing at my mouth. I groaned and grabbed him. The truck door swung in and knocked me on the legs—I knew it would leave a bruise—but I didn't care. I pressed him back onto the seat.

When I licked down his neck, I got a tongue full of pond goo. Yech. I stood up and his face registered disappointment. "What's wrong?" he asked.

"How about a little mini-shower? I've got some water in the back."

"Sure." He sat up, his long, pink cock bonging against his belly. Nice.

I reached in my truck bed and set my five-gallon watercooler on the side so that the spigot was over the edge. He had to bend down to get under the trickle. "Got any soap?" he asked.

"Just this." I pawed in the glove compartment and gave him one of those small soaps you get in motels, handy when you get filthy on the job.

"Aren't you gonna help me out?" He washed his face and neck and I nibbled at him.

"I'll give you more than some help." He washed and I rinsed him down, using a Wendy's cup left from dinner the night before. The water made him shiver. I watched it trickle down his chest and over his belly button, drip down his beautiful, pale cock. As I looked, it filled and rose. It turned from cream to rich pink and it reached up toward me, bobbing in the morning air.

I grabbed the soap and held his gaze while I cleaned his cock. Its skin was soft against my calloused palm, bouncing as I wrapped my hand around it. The suds made him so slippery that I lost my grip a couple of times as I jerked him off. He leaned against the truck, the water trickling down his torso, and as the suds were washed away, my hand tightened on his cock. His head dropped back, his mouth open and wanting, and I grabbed harder, pulling with each stroke. With my other hand I cupped his balls, stroking and tugging in time with my jerks on him.

As I watched, his beautiful cock changed color, from pink to deep wine as blood rushed through it. I felt his balls draw up, tightening a little, and then he gasped. His fingers gripped my upper arms and he cried out, "Oh fuck yes! Yes!" He came, gushing wet spurts of creamy semen. It glistened in the sunlight, a silvery sheen in the puddles of water around us. The first shot splashed up on his chest. The next few went into the air and landed on his belly. I kept up with a few more strokes and felt his cock soften in my hand.

"Oh, man. You've got some smooth moves there." His voice was whispery, a little shaky.

"I've got more smooth right here," I said, grabbing my own cock. I turned him around and pushed him against the passenger seat. His ass was round, the cheeks pale and smooth, not a trace of hair. I gripped his cheeks from below, playing, kneading. I used my thumbs to pull his cheeks apart and he squirmed in my grip. He thrust back and forth against the seat, moaning. As I played with him, I saw the gator on the bank move. Away? Was I going to lose him?

But seeing Paul bent over the truck's seat, ass pushed out, my hard-on straining at my khakis, I wasn't about to stop. Mr. Gator would hang around the neighborhood. Paul? Maybe wouldn't.

Out of the corner of my eye, I saw the gator settle down and go back to sleep. He'd been shifting to expose the other side of his body to the sun. Paul pressed his butt against my fingers, turned his head to plant a wet half kiss against my chin. "You got some protection, doncha?"

"In the glove box."

Paul fumbled through fast-food napkins, straws, and a box of shotgun shells, and found the lube and condoms. I grabbed the lube, smeared some on my fingers. Paul's asscrack was light brown and then pink just outside his hole. Dark red fuzz wisped around his anus and I wet it with lube. I tickled him, using one finger, just inside him a little, then out.

Paul groaned and pushed backward. "Please!"

"No more yapping!" I leaned down, let my weight sink against him. I rubbed my hard cock against his ass, watching the khaki fabric tease at his skin, feeling my shorts tight against my hard-on. "I'll fuck you when I'm good and ready."

I slipped one lubed finger inside him, pushing past his band of muscle, feeling it loosen and then let me in. Oh, bliss. He clamped down, gasping. He was tight and warm and damn, I wanted to spear into him. But that wasn't how it was in my fantasies, so I made myself slow down.

Enjoy it, take my time.

Paul panted on the seat in front of me. Birds sang from the trees and from a distance I heard a lawnmower grumble. The gator slept on the edge of the pond. All around us the morning moseyed on while I was about to fuck one of the most gorgeous guys I'd ever seen.

My zipper was loud. My cock popped out of my shorts before I even pulled them down. The air was cool, easing over my cock, up under my shirt, between my legs. I gave my balls a gentle roll as I freed them. Paul twisted to look down. "Nice dick, dude."

"It'll be nicer up your ass." I stroked it a few times, a rough, steady pull. Paul's face and neck flushed and he groaned.

"My turn," Paul said. He turned to face me. He was damp from sweat and the little shower he'd taken. His mouth opened. His long, pink cock grew again as I watched it. That made me even harder, knowing he was hot again, that I'd made him respond. He gripped my cock with warm fingers, teasing. I moaned. He gave me a quick half smile, then kept his gaze down as he worked on me. The sound of skin on skin seemed loud, a *whish-whish* of friction and pleasure. "You're hot, man, so fucking hot."

"Don't stop," I whispered. He eased one palm under my balls, kneading and twisting. He looked up then, and pushed one finger to just the right spot behind my balls. His finger circled and rubbed, circled and rubbed.

"Oh, yeah, right there," I moaned.

Blood filled my groin. The sounds of the morning faded away—all I could hear was our panting and the stroke of his hand on me. Precum slicked his hand. It tightened on my cock.

"I'm gonna come if you keep going. Get me covered, pretty boy. It's time to fuck."

The condom felt cool but his fingers were warm as he tugged it over me. I smelled the condom—that faintly medicinal odor—and I smelled Paul, the real scent of his skin beneath the soap. I nipped at his ear and neck as he got the rubber set. "Ready, big boy?" he asked.

"I hope you're ready, pretty boy," I growled and turned him around—hard. He winced as his knees hit the edge of the truck floor, but then he bent over the seat, showing me that glorious ass, and I didn't care.

His wet skin made a slick sound against the vinyl seat. My knees were jammed against the metal of the doorframe—more bruises, but I didn't care. I grabbed his ass and spread his cheeks apart, thumbing between them, making him groan. His hole winked at me as I stretched him apart.

Nice. More than nice.

One of my billy clubs rolled off the seat as Paul squirmed around. I grabbed it and his gaze followed my hand as I played with the hunk of metal. "I keep this around to put animals out of their misery." I stroked it around his shoulders and alongside his neck. Paul rubbed his face on it. The black metal looked nasty against his freckled cheeks—deeper than naughty, dirty.

Hot.

"Just fuck me, hillbilly boy and shut up." His voice was hoarse and he sounded mean. Annoyed. He pressed back and my cock bonged up against his ass.

I slipped my cock between his cheeks and clamped them together with my hands. The wet of the condom made it slippery and milky and Paul panted as I teased him, moving up and down, feeling his warm flesh against me. I slipped the billy club between his cheeks, too. "Which do you want, pretty boy? The club or me?"

"You!"

"Beg me," I ordered.

"Fuck me," he panted back. "Please fuck me!"

I teased him—and myself—some more. My cock thudded up against his cheeks, thrusting around, looking for a home. I spread his cheeks again and put the head just inside. Paul groaned again and pushed backward. "Come on!" he bawled. "Fuck me, you fucking cock tease!"

It was time. I pushed up inside him, feeling my own buttcheeks clench together as I thrust in. He was tight—lubed open, but still young enough to be tight and warm. The feel of his warmth past the condom was sexy as hell. I pushed in as far as I could, my balls rubbing up against his. The truck's old chassis shifted as I stroked in and out of him, the seat squeaking a little as I pumped into him. The billy club fell to the floor again, forgotten.

Paul rubbed his own cock on the seat as I fucked him. He gave a breathy, "Oh, oh, oh," with every thrust of my cock inside him. His face was wet with water and sweat and his mouth stayed open. "Oh, right there, get me right there!" he groaned. I gave a twisting thrust and that must have worked. His whole back tensed, his shoulders bent back and he raised his head as he cried out again. "Oh, god, Denny, fuck me till I come. Fuck me!" One more angled thrust and he came. He tightened down on my cock, spasms of his own orgasm connecting to me and I felt myself getting closer. My cock heated up, thickened even more, and my balls drew up.

I felt Paul relax in my grip. He turned his head, catching a glimpse of me working him. His eyes got dark. "Are you close?" he asked, huffing with each word because of me thrusting into him.

"Yeah," I managed to whisper.

He reached down, grabbed the billy club in one hand and held it to his mouth. His smile was dark. He kissed the black metal, watching me. Then he licked the billy club, his pink tongue working over the metal, up and down. That did it.

I bent over him, biting his neck and shoulders. I couldn't stop my groans; I just growled and fucked him faster and harder, faster and harder.

"Come in me, Denny!"

The world narrowed to my cock. The fire and heat of coming made my knees loosen a little. With one last groan, I shot into him, the waves of orgasm spurting from my cock. My breathing turned into gasps and I grabbed his hips and pushed further into him. I fell onto him, my chest covering his damp back, his asscheeks warm against my groin.

Our heavy breathing filled the truck cab. I heard the birds outside again and the silly quack of cormorant out on the pond. I was too happy where I was to worry if Mr. Gator was still outside, so I just lay on Paul's back until I was completely soft. He turned to kiss me again, one of those awkward half kisses, and I pulled away reluctantly.

I tugged the condom off and my pants up. Paul turned to me, looking sexy as hell. We grinned at each other.

"Thanks for the welcome to Florida," he said, and kissed me again, for real this time.

"You're more than welcome. We always like to keep the tourists happy," I said. "You got a number here I can call you at?"

"Sure." He jotted down a phone number on the back of one of my business cards.

"I gotta get this gator caught. I'll call you tonight." I smiled. "Maybe I can find another way to use that billy club on you."

"You've got enough club for me."

We got dressed and just as Paul left, I saw the gator slip back into the pond. Eight hundred dollars' worth of reptile. Gone.

But I smiled anyway.

HOT EATS

Kal Cobalt

Near midnight, my diner shifted from quiet to dead silent. Darlene's shift was over, and I'd sent Barry home early to tell his wife goodnight. The standard graveyard-shift crowd—freight-train railroaders from the depot across the street who liked their burgers well done and their steak with A-1—had come and gone.

The first customer after Barry left was a tall, rangy man in a gray T-shirt streaked with dirt. He greeted me with the cautious smile of the truly exhausted, though I could tell he was no railroader: no grime under the fingernails, no heavy bag of on-the-road necessities. "I didn't think there'd be anyplace open," he said, sliding his narrow ass onto one of my counter stools.

"We're open till two." I poured a hot cup of coffee for him, unasked.

"Thanks." He sipped at it, then looked up at me with slightly wider eyes. "Fresh."

I nodded. "We treat graveyarders right."

"I think you just secured yourself a regular."

"Good to know." I slipped him a menu. "Pies are half off after midnight."

"Definitely a regular, then." He wore the same kind of black-rimmed glasses Barry did, although I suspected they were at least twice as expensive.

"What would bring you here regularly in the middle of the night? You don't work the rails."

He shook his head. "Film. I lens the production shooting in the valley."

"You lens it? Cameraman?"

"Sort of. Cinematographer. Lord of the cameramen," he grinned, wrapping long, ropy fingers around the coffee mug. "Lord of the night shoots, too. It's hell down there."

"Sounds like hard work."

"Grueling work. I'm starved." He eyed the menu, flipping its single laminated page over. "You guys do the fried chicken this late?"

"If you'll take mashed on the side."

"I was going to ask for that. And the corn, please."

"Sure thing." I'd seen Barry assemble that plate often enough. I headed back to the kitchen, smiling to myself, and then it hit me: *Shit. I like him.* What little sex life I had, I kept separate from the diner scrupulously, and from the whole town of Grange if I could manage it. I barely broke even as it was, and the slightest whiff of homosexuality would drive the hard-working, big-tipping railroader crowd off me faster than a failed health inspection.

"What's your name?" I asked when I brought out the stranger's plate.

"Ted."

"Nice to meet you, Ted."

"Are you the owner?" he asked, ripping meat off the chicken breast with gusto.

"I am."

"You still get stuck with graveyard, huh? Can't find someone reliable to take it?"

"I prefer it. I'd keep the place open all night if I could."

Ted gave a surprised little nod. "So you could have any shift you want, but you pick nights. And I can't have any shift but nights on this production, and I hate them."

"I think life thinks that's funny."

Ted snorted agreement. "I think you're right. Life's got one hell of a sense of humor."

You're telling me. "I'm just going to start wrapping up the pies. Should I leave one out for you?"

"Slice of key lime, please," he said around a mouthful of mashed.

It was ridiculous to think I could intuit something about a man based on his dinner, but that didn't stop me from entertaining the notion. I speculated that this was not his traditional diet; he was far too lean and ropy to exist on fried foods and pie. Then again, if the dirt stains on his T-shirt were any indication, he worked hard; that, combined with irregular meals and a fast metabolism, might allow him to manage it all.

I shook my head. I'd had some strange flights of fancy while wrapping up the pies night after night, but this one took the cake. So to speak.

"Are you the only graveyard grub around here?" Ted asked. "Not that I'm going to jump ship, I just wonder. Everything else seems closed up tight."

"Everything else closes at ten, unless you want a bar."

Ted grunted. "Flashback to childhood. I grew up in a small town like this."

"Yeah?"

"I probably would've stayed, too, except that it's hard to make a living as a cinematographer in a town of ten thousand."

I nodded. "It's more suited to diners than movies." And more suited to people with conservative sex lives; that Ted grew up in a small town and wished he still lived in one didn't bode well for my attraction, and I made myself tune out after that. I feigned exhaustion on a par with Ted's and pretended I liked to get all the cleanup done before I closed. I tried, very hard, not to watch the way he stuck his tongue out slightly to receive every forkful of key lime pie, and gave him only the standard thanks-and-good-bye nod when he stood. He left a good tip.

I convinced myself he was none the wiser, and I'd almost rid myself of my attraction to him. That lasted right up until I slid into bed, when I envisioned him on his knees in front of me, his mouth open, his tongue stuck out slightly to receive my cock.

"How are things with the wife?"

Barry eyed me over the rims of his glasses as he washed his hands. "Nothing new to report."

I nodded, trying to seem casual. Ted had been in every night for five nights, enjoying Barry's far superior fried chicken, and every night for five nights I'd tried to be just friendly enough, hoping neither Ted nor Barry would suspect me. Tonight, if Ted came in, it would be his night off; we'd have time to talk, I thought, and maybe—just maybe—I'd see some glimmer of interest from him. "Want to knock off early?" I asked Barry as smoothly as I could.

Barry grunted. "Not sure that'll make any difference. She yells no matter when I get home."

I pointed at the slightly wilted spray of wildflowers in an empty milk jug that a sixth-grade class had offered me as a tip. "Take those with you, see if she yells."

Barry dried his hands and gave me a sideways look. "Your marriage counseling isn't exactly subtle."

I patted him on the back. "Your personality demands straightforwardness."

"Mmm. Don't work too hard." He picked up his jacket, eyed me a little, and took the wildflowers, too. "If I still get yelled at, I'm blaming you."

"I'd expect nothing less."

The diner fell into an eerie quiet in Barry's absence. I watched the clock. Ted only got one night off a week, he'd told me, and slowly I realized that without the stricture of a meal period, he could cook something himself, back at his hotel. Or eat early and catch up on sleep. There were a dozen reasons he wouldn't walk through my door.

Instead, he was later than usual; he wandered in at one forty-five, sheepish behind his black rims. "Any chance of grub?"

"For you? Sure." I reached for the coffeepot.

"None of that tonight, thanks. I've got to sleep."

I nodded. "Beer?"

"Perfect."

"Bud?"

"You know me well."

I knew him well enough to risk what I was about to do, at least. I had no liquor license, and had suggested Bud simply because I had a couple of bottles stashed in the fridge for myself. "On the house," I told him, and came around the counter to turn the sign to CLOSED and lock the door.

Ted grinned. "My lips are sealed."

"Thanks. The usual?"

"Yes, please."

As I fried the chicken, I pondered how to approach him. Beer rather than coffee was a good sign, but it was still dicey. I figured he wouldn't exactly run out to ruin my reputation now, but I risked losing his casual friendship if I spoke up. Then again, if we felt the same way about each other, he was probably out there thinking the same thing.

"How's that sitting?" I asked, nodding toward his beer when I brought out his dinner.

"Very well, thanks." He tore into the chicken breast first, as usual, and made panicky little huffing sounds as he sucked air into his mouth to cool off that first searing bite, as usual.

I watched him eat. I could say something, anything, to get the dialogue started, especially now that he was committed to the meal and a more or less captive audience. Especially now that he was licking the buttery mashed potatoes off his fork. Especially when he wrapped his lips around the beer bottle so perfectly.

I fetched his slice of pie instead, my cheeks hot.

"You're quiet tonight," Ted noted.

"Preoccupied."

"If you want to talk, I'll listen. You've listened to me whine often enough." Ted licked a stray streak of butter from the corner of his mouth.

"Not sure you'd be interested in what's on my mind."

He gave me a come-hither motion with one greasy-fingered hand. "Try me."

I stared at him, trying to convince myself to speak. "Relationship problems," I finally said.

He laughed. "I can definitely lend an ear to those."

"It's not like that. It's not knowing if how I feel about someone is reciprocated."

"There's a good way to find out." He sucked an especially greasy finger into his mouth.

"Yeah?"

"Mmm-hmm. Ask."

I shook my head. "Good idea, wrong situation."

"Mmm. Sensitive arrangement?"

"You could say that."

"You could drop hints. You know, hang around a little more than you have to. Be friendly. Stop by for dinner, even on the nights when you're not working."

I blinked. "Are you serious?"

Ted shrugged.

I fought with myself over what would be better: confess attraction to him, or just my orientation? Pros, cons, and my moment slipping away. "I'm gay," I said, my cheeks hot.

"I'm bi." Ted's voice was completely level, his gaze firm.

Oh, god. "I'm attracted to you."

Ted grinned. "Your fried chicken's nothing compared to Barry's. Why do you think I keep coming back?"

I laughed. Just shook my head and laughed. "Well, thank you. And I know. About the fried chicken."

Ted shrugged. "Your conversation makes up for it. And your ass." He wiped his hands thoroughly on his napkin, grinning at me. "Can I have a tour of the kitchen?"

"Come on in." I beckoned for him to come around the counter.

He got to his feet, offering me a sly smile. "Always wondered what it was like back there."

I pushed open the double doors and made a wide Vanna White gesture. "Welcome to the kitchen. Here's the standing freezer—"

"Stop right there. I like the standing freezer." He backed me against it, his big, wiry hands tight on my hip bone.

I swallowed. This close, I could smell the fried chicken on his breath, the warm tang of his sweat. He just watched me, lips curved slightly upward, waiting for me. There were windows. We could be seen. My reputation—

Fuck my reputation.

I slid my hands up the sides of his face and gently pulled his glasses off, resting them on the top of the freezer. I'd seen him without his glasses once before, on a bad night, when he'd pulled them off to rub at his eye sockets with the heel of his hand; seeing his eyes this way was much more satisfying. I pulled him toward me, tilting my head to place a kiss on his upturned lips.

The first touch was electric. His mouth opened immediately for my tongue, his hips arching up for me at the same time. I wrapped one arm around his waist, dragging him against me, but he shoved me back, pinning me against the cool exterior of the freezer.

"Goddamn," he moaned against my mouth. "Why the hell didn't you say something sooner?"

"I could ask you the same thing." I slid my hands along his belt, easing the tongue out of the buckle.

"Small town. Not a good place to go professing attraction for boys," Ted grinned, tugging my shirt out of my jeans.

"Same here." I yanked Ted's zipper down, shoved my hand down his Calvins. His cock was thick and heavy already, a hot moist heft below crisp, dark curls. His hips bucked toward me uncontrollably, and I grinned and made a fist for him to thrust into.

"Not enough." Ted pulled the bar apron from around my waist and dropped it to the floor, then tore into my slacks with a hunger I hadn't seen in him, even for Barry's fried chicken.

"Not enough," I agreed. In moments his jeans were around his thighs and my slacks were at my ankles, my ass cold against the freezer door.

"I suppose the health department doesn't look too kindly on this kind of thing," Ted moaned against my mouth, his rough hand wrapping around my cock.

"Health department guy's on vacation." I grabbed Ted's ass, dragged him hard against me. "I'll clean up, promise."

"Suck me off?" Ted bit at my neck, just below my ear, and words failed me.

I moaned instead and slid to my knees, my discarded apron cushioning them from the cracked linoleum floor. Ted's cock bobbed upward in anticipation, and I wrapped my lips around the head, humming softly at the dark, salty taste of him.

"Fuck," Ted moaned, leaning forward to brace his forearms on the freezer. "Won't last."

I pulled back, rubbing my hand over his spit-slick cock. "Don't want you to." I took him deep then, wrapping my arms around his waist. I heard his fingers claw at the lid of the freezer, so fucking hot, and kept going as quickly as I could.

Ted cupped one strong, calloused hand around the back of my head, and I opened wide to receive his thrusts all the way into the back of my throat. His groans echoed off the walls of the tiny kitchen as he came, hot salty jets across the back of my tongue, and I closed my eyes as I swallowed him down.

"Christ," he breathed, clinging to the freezer as he backed up to let me off my knees. "That was really good."

I kissed him lightly, still savoring the taste of him in my mouth. "It was."

Ted gave me a sudden, boyish grin, pressing me up tight against the freezer. "Ever been sucked off in your diner before?"

"Uh—no," I gasped, shuddering at the way his hip bone was snugged just so against my cock, "but if you keep coming around I'll be happy to—make it a habit...."

Ted snorted out a little laugh, leaning down to brush a kiss against my lips. "Me too." He pressed closer, forcing my ass firmly against the cool freezer, and slid one hand down over my cock.

"Fuck—won't last long," I groaned, shifting so I could wrap my hand around his.

"Mmm. Show me." Ted leaned his hand up gently into mine.

So I did: I gripped his hand and showed him how to stroke me, tight and long. There was a certain lightness to his eyes, a joy in the playful aspects of our situation even as he worked hard to drive me completely out of my mind. He leaned down over me, brushing his lips against my ear. "Wanted you from the first time," he panted. "Thought about bending you over the counter and having to untie your little apron before I unbuckled your belt." He slid down to his knees, and I braced my arm against the wall behind the freezer in preparation.

"Wanted to suck you off right there on the barstool," I offered in return, barely breathing. His lips nearly touched my cockhead. I felt his breath against my slit.

Ted gave me another one of those brilliant, half-crazy smiles. "No reason we can't do all of the above," he said, and sucked me down.

It was like Ted's mouth was made for my cock. He hollowed his cheeks, playing his tongue up along the underside and teasing the spot where the shaft met the cockhead. I tangled my fingers in his hair, watching him find a slow, steady rhythm. He cupped my balls in one hand, teasing behind them gently with his fingertips, and my knees buckled. "Close," I hitched out.

He pulled back, fondling my balls firmly. "I had a feeling," he smirked, and set to sucking me as hard and fast as I'd ever been treated to before.

"Oh, god," I groaned, rising up on my toes, working my hips forward in time to the sucking, smacking passes of his mouth. My balls tightened in his hand, and with one last moan I came, holding his head close, thrusting my cock along his tongue as spasm after spasm wracked me and he swallowed every drop.

I sagged against the freezer, completely spent. Ted got to his feet, his hands on my hips, and nuzzled into my neck. "Damn, I needed that," he grinned, kissing me on the lips. "You all right?"

"Yeah." I nodded toward the windows out to the darkened street; in the distance, the streetlights blinked yellow. "Hoping the cop doesn't see the lights on after closing and check up on me."

"Mmm. D'you have a bathroom where we can clean up?"

"Yeah." I pushed away from the freezer, picking up my slacks just to carry them in front of me modestly as I led the way to the tiny employee-only washroom.

"That's better," Ted murmured, and pressed me tight against the wall beside the toilet, kissing me hungrily.

I grunted, startled, but quickly returned the kiss, dropping my slacks to drag him closer by his still-open jeans. He slid those big hands around the small of my back, crushing me against him until his tongue was down my throat and I could barely breathe. When he pulled back, it was only far enough to look into my eyes. His lips quirked up fondly, and he carded the tips of his fingers through my hair.

"Is Barry working tomorrow night?"

I grinned. "No. Morning shift."

"Good. See you for a quickie?"

"Absolutely."

I breezed into the diner the following afternoon with a huge grin. There was no point in trying to hide it; I was pretty sure I'd even smiled in my sleep. "How's business?" I asked Barry.

"Booming. Hey, question for you." He rested a pair of black-rimmed glasses on the counter.

I glanced at him; he was still wearing his. "What are those?"

"Found them on the floor by the freezer."

I swallowed. "Oh."

Barry shook his head. "Listen, you know I don't mind the night shift too much. If you want me to take one so you two can use an actual bed sometime, I would."

I blinked. "What?"

He lowered his head, staring at me mock-accusingly over the rims of his glasses. "It wasn't hard to piece together, even before these." He waved the glasses. "You've never been this interested in my marriage before. Marilyn says hi, by the way, and thanks for the flowers."

"Uh." I looked away, trying to ignore the sinking feeling in my stomach. "I guess I figured you'd be against that kind of thing."

Barry shrugged. "You must want it pretty bad if you're getting it on in the kitchen. It's none of my business anyway, but it's not like I can't relate, too."

I shook my head again. "Well, thanks. I didn't expect this."

"I have a feeling you didn't expect him, either," Barry winked. "You let me go home a few hours and rest up, and I'll come back before your fella gets here."

"Thank you, Barry."

"You're welcome." He winked again, wiping his hands on his apron. "Don't forget: we're not *all* conservative around here."

"BROKEBACK MOUNTAIN"

Simon Sheppard

They'd grown up together, Perry and Tom, in the same little backwater town in north-central Florida, a spot far enough from Disney World to still be an outpost of proud, self-proclaimed crackers. Back in high school, skinny, awkward Perry had had a crush on Tom, who'd been on the football team and seemed unafraid of anything. But it wasn't till they graduated—Perry with honors, Tom pretty much just scraping through—that Perry had dared speak up.

It was the end of a stifling July afternoon, expected thunderstorms not having arrived, and they were parked out in the middle of nowhere, the two of them in Perry's dad's pickup, sharing a joint and staring toward the sun setting garishly over the flat, heat-seared horizon. It was 1989.

"Jesus," Tom said, exhaling a cloud of smoke, "I can't stand sticking around this cracker town any longer than I have to."

"Nothing wrong with being a cracker," Perry said, then inhaled, paused, exhaled. "But I'm gonna miss you, buddy." Why the fuck had he said that? Why? Fucking sentimental fool.

"Nah, I'm getting out," Tom said, "as soon as I can. Perry?"

"Yeah?"

"I got accepted to a college in Colorado. Football scholarship. And I'm going." A long pause. "But I'll miss you, too."

Perry let the smoke out. He was feeling like he'd had enough. "You're kidding."

"And why would I be kidding you?" Tom took the joint from Perry's trembling hand and took a deep hit. Then he reached his right hand over, touched Perry's face and turned it toward his.

"Tom..." Perry began. "I..."

Tom leaned over, placed his mouth on Perry's, felt his friend's lips open, and slowly exhaled a stream of smoke into Perry's mouth.

Perry took the smoke in, feeling his chest expand, his heart pound, his dick get hard, so hard. He recycled the pot smoke back into Tom's lungs, then let his tongue find his buddy's.

The sun had set, it was dark; there was not much of anything around, not even orange groves. Anybody driving by would announce his presence with oncoming headlights in plenty of time. Safe, kind of. Still kissing, Tom let his hand trail downward, over Perry's T-shirt, down to the bulge in his jeans. Perry, for his part, having dreamed so long of just such a moment, still felt scared and more than a little giddy, though some—a lot—of that might have been due to the grass. Nevertheless, he decided to help out, reaching down and unzipping his own fly. Tom's fingers burrowed their way inside, pressing on Perry's hard-on through his rapidly moistening briefs.

It felt amazing.

Tom ended the kiss, leaving a trickle of drool running down Perry's chin. He undid Perry's pants, tugged the tattered white cotton briefs down over his friend's thin thighs, and Perry's damp, uncut dick sprang forth, into the humid Southern air.

"Oh my god, Tom!" Perry gasped, feeling his cock being enveloped by Tom's mouth. "Oh, sweet Jesus." And then, suddenly, everything screamed to resolution, Perry pumping a big load of sperm into Tom's mouth, and all the while, Clint Black was singing on the radio.

Tom leaned out of the open window and spat out his pal's sperm. A car's headlights were heading their way, but the deed was already done.

"You better straighten yourself up, buddy," Tom said. "You've gotta drive me home."

That was the beginning of it. Perry and Tom sucked each other off a lot that burning summer, and Perry, unlike his friend, liked to swallow. One weekend, when they both had time off from their lousy jobs, Perry was able to borrow his father's pickup and they drove all the way to Panama City, where they rented the cheapest motel room they could find. That was where Tom fucked Perry for the first time, the first-timer pain softened by illegal beer and a couple of hits of good grass. It was tough for Perry to take it while he was lying on his back, so he straddled Tom's football-player body and rode his dick, bouncing breathlessly up and down, feeling his guts being stretched by hard flesh, his own erect cock standing straight up, leaking juice, until they both, within seconds of each other, came.

Afterward, they pulled on their swimsuits and headed out to the beach. Lying on the powdery sand, watching Tom run into the surf, his husky body shining with seawater, it occurred to Perry that he'd never felt happier.

There was, really, only one complication to their secret bliss. Carrie. She'd been Perry's girlfriend through most of high school (the two of them enduring countless "Perry and Carrie" jokes) and she'd chosen the night of their senior prom to inform Perry that she was pregnant and would not, no never, "kill the baby." Though Perry had been a pretty good student—especially in English, where his writing skills shone—his family couldn't afford to send him off to college. So he'd figured on a couple of years at community college, and then maybe a transfer to somewhere else. And now the prospect of a kid put all that into question.

Sure, Perry was almost certain that he loved Carrie, and he enjoyed fucking her, or at least he had before pregnancy came into the picture. So if her birth-control pills had failed, well, he would do the honorable thing and marry her. But for now, this one last summer of equivocal freedom, he would get stoned and drunk and let Tom fuck him and not say a word about Carrie...unless asked.

And, at last, Tom did ask him. Maybe he hadn't mentioned her earlier because he really didn't want to know. "Hey, what's happening with Carrie?" he said, one night in late July.

"I'm getting married to her, I guess. She's expecting. We're getting married before the kid comes." Despite his facility in English, Perry wasn't one to varnish the facts.

"Wow," Tom said. "Wow. I was hoping that maybe someday..."

He sounded unexpectedly emotional. But Perry thought that Tom—the one who'd be leaving in just over a month—had no right to be upset. Things were the way things were. He rolled over, scooched down, and took Tom's cock back into his mouth. It tasted saltily of Tom's recent orgasm, but even so, it started getting hard again within seconds.

Things just were the way things were.

Carrie lost the baby soon after she and Perry got married. It was the first of a series of disappointments, but then, Perry knew, life was really just one damn letdown after another. As the months, and then the years, crept by, he sometimes thought back to those couple of relatively carefree months after high school when he and Tom had all that fun. And he remembered—at night, usually, as he lay in bed next to his sleeping wife—the taste of Tom's dick, how Tom felt inside him. Oh well, those days were gone forever. He wasn't really queer, he knew, it was just a fling between friends.

Oh, sure, there had been a couple of other moments. Once, when he was drinking a beer at the Last Stop Bar, he'd met a trucker whose rig had broken down outside town, and they ended up back at the trucker's motel room, more than half-drunk, the burly trucker barely able to get his big, smelly dick hard inside Perry's mouth; Perry, not having any erection problems himself, eventually got bored, jacked off, and left. And stuff had happened a couple of other times, too. But mostly, he was faithful to Carrie. Mostly.

At first, Tom had sent him letters every once in a while, letting him know how he was doing in school in Colorado, telling Perry how much he missed him. Perry would write back, with not much news to report, never getting as emotional as Tom seemed to be. What, after all, would be the point? He was married, he was a redneck boy, and Carrie, after a lot of trying, was pregnant again. He never told Tom about that last thing, though, and when Tom sent a letter saying, "You should really come out here, Per. There are mountains, real mountains like you've never seen," Perry never got around to writing a reply. There were a couple more letters from Tom, increasingly pleading, and then the notes stopped coming.

They named the baby Lisa Marie.

Lisa Marie was four when Perry heard from Tom again. It was surprising news, really. Tom had been on the verge of flunking out of college when he met a country-rock band that had come to play a concert at his school. They'd needed a roadie, so Tom had signed on, moved to Los Angeles, and—apparently—now spelled his name "Thom." The band had gone through a fallow period when the original guitarist had overdosed and nearly died, then gone through rehab, then relapsed. But with their new guitarist—one who could keep his eyes open on stage—they'd scored a big hit, one Perry had found himself humming along to whenever it was on the radio. Now they were going on a nationwide tour, and they'd be playing in Orlando in about a month. Would it be okay if Thom came north on a visit?

"Oh, sure, bud!" Perry wrote back, right away. "It would be great to see you."

The week before Thom was due to arrive, Perry found himself uncommonly happy. Even Carrie noticed the difference. "You've lost that hangdog look," she said. "Guess you're excited to see your old friend, huh?" She'd known Thom, of course, but had never much liked him.

When Thom showed up, he was maybe fifteen pounds heavier, and his hair was a lot longer. But it was still the same old Tom, only with an *h*. Carrie had cooked dinner for them, and they all sat around talking somewhat awkwardly, Perry barely able to control his thoughts. At last, when Carrie was in the kitchen getting dessert, Thom leaned over and whispered, "So how about it, Perry? Want to go out and get hammered and talk over old times?"

Perry just nodded. "Hey babe," he said, when Carrie returned with the Bundt cake, "Hope you don't mind, but Thom and I are gonna go out and have a few drinks, catch up on things. We'll probably be late, so don't wait up." He tried to keep his tone as controlled as possible, and, scrutinize as he might, he couldn't spot a trace of suspicion on his wife's face.

"So when Mama got sick, I quit community college so I could take care of her. I figured being an English teacher wasn't all that great an idea, anyhow."

"And now?" Thom asked.

"I work at a stable over at Ocala." That was where rich folks kept their horses, something for their daughters to do on weekends. "It's kind of a long commute, but I like the job, and it pays pretty good." He didn't bother telling Thom that the middle-aged businessman who owned the horses sometimes paid Perry generously for rides that had nothing to do with horses.

"Well, I guess life threw us both a few curves." Thom put his hand firmly on Perry's thigh. It was all Perry could do to keep the truck from swerving off the road.

Might as well just say it, since his dick had been hard ever since they'd gotten into the pickup. "Thom, you just thirsty? Or are you horny?"

"What do you think?" His hand traveled upward and gave Perry's well-remembered hard-on a squeeze. "Well, I guess I don't have to ask *you* that."

They wound up in the same cheap motel where Perry had sucked the fat, soft dick of the drunken trucker. They opened the bottle of bourbon that Thom had bought and swigged it down from the plastic glasses that had been standing, wrapped in cellophane, next to the not-very-clean sink.

"Man, I've thought so much about this," Thom said.

Perry felt slightly uneasy and somewhat drunk. "Let me suck your cock," he said.

Thom's prick was hefty and hard and it filled Perry's mouth

up with masculine flesh. Jesus, it was good to be sucking it. He felt Thom's hand on his head, stroking his hair. Thom said something under his breath that might have been "breaking my heart," something like that. Perry wasn't sure how he was supposed to react, so he just kept on sucking.

"Hey, back off. I'm real close," Thom said. Perry did, his friend's swollen dickhead just inches away. But cum was already drooling from Thom's piss slit, and with a spasm, the thick cock started to shoot. Before Perry was able to get his mouth back on it, a spurt landed on his hair, but he got to gulp the rest of it down.

"Fuck, that felt great," Thom said, after he'd caught his breath. "You have no idea how often I've thought of that."

Perry just knelt there, his hard-on still in his jeans.

"You want to get off?" Thom asked.

"Maybe later."

"So you want to just lie around and talk?"

"Sure."

They stripped naked and got into the saggy bed. They lay there, side by side, drinking bourbon, not saying very much. Thom rolled onto his side and started stroking Perry's lanky, stretched-out body. His fingertips moved from Perry's Adam's apple, over the curve of his neck, his chest; touched a nipple, squeezed it; then ran over the dark blond hair of Perry's belly, down to his bush, his hard dick. He grabbed that cock, held on to it for dear life, and felt his own shaft hardening again.

Soon Thom was on top of Perry, grinding his hard-on against his buddy's. But when he spread Perry legs and began caressing his warm asshole, Perry spoke up.

"Hey, uh," he said, somewhat woozily, "I really don't think, with my wife and all, that you should..."

"Hang on." Thom rolled off Perry and reached over for his

tour jacket. Fishing in the pocket, he pulled out a rubber and a little packet of lube.

"You came prepared," said Perry, "didn'cha?"

It hurt a little when Thom entered him—he hadn't been fucked in a while—but he soon relaxed into the delicious feeling of his friend thrusting away inside him. He tried to keep his hand away from his own dick, focus on nothing but Thom's pleasure. But eventually he had to say it: "You mind if I come?"

"Course not. You been waiting awhile."

Perry's orgasm was intense, and then Thom pulled out, stroked himself just a few times, and filled up the greasy rubber with his own milky cum, spurt after spurt into the translucent tip.

When they'd showered and gotten dressed, they decided to go for a walk, maybe sober up some before driving back to Perry's. The motel was on the edge of what town there was, and it didn't take long before they were walking through a dimly lit field, the crescent moon being socked in behind thick clouds. The crickets were loud. Thom reached for Perry's hand and gave it a squeeze. Perry squeezed back. As they stood there, silent, hand in hand, there was a zigzag flash of lightning, illuminating cypress and saw palmetto, and seconds later a crash of thunder. A small explosion in the sky.

"Jesus," Thom said. "Jesus."

Getting back to his house a couple of hours before dawn, Perry crawled into bed with his wife to steal what sleep he could before he had to get up and drive to Ocala for work. Thom passed out, slumped and snoring, in the backseat of his car, parked beside Perry's truck. By the time Perry climbed into his pickup, the rain had stopped and Thom's Ford was gone, leaving nothing but a dry patch on the blacktop.

The years, as they always do, passed. The Grammy-nominated country-rock outfit Thom worked for dissolved in a thicket of lawsuits and recriminations, but he, by that time a known quantity on the roadie circuit, soon found employment with a heavy metal band whose fans tended to wear T-shirts with satanic symbols. They toured quite a lot, so Thom and Perry saw each other an average of two or three times a year. Usually they were just alone for an hour or two, though a couple of times Perry was able to go off on weekend trips with his buddy, camping trips that turned into outdoor sex once the sun went down. Thom invited his friend out to L.A., but Perry couldn't figure out a graceful excuse to give both his job and his wife, and besides, as he wrote Thom, *I'm just a good old boy who hasn't even visited Disney, much less the other coast.* Eventually, that changed; he took his growing daughter and thickening wife on a trip to the Magic Kingdom, and Thom flew in from Georgia for the occasion, the two men sharing a couple of torrid hours in a hotel on International Drive.

That night in Orlando was the first time Perry had fucked Thom, instead of vice versa. Perry had long ago gotten over any squeamishness he'd had over sex that involved the butthole. That evening, sliding his cock into his buddy's hairy crack, he realized how much tighter ass was than pussy, and was glad for the pleasure he'd provided Thom all those times when Thom had been the one doing the screwing. Perry fucked Thom every which way, including some he'd never tried with Carrie. Standing up. From behind, like a bitch. Face-to-face, like they were lovers. Thom had more trouble staying hard while he got fucked, but he managed to whip a load out of himself while Perry was still inside him. Only after he saw Thom's belly drenched in sperm did Perry let go and come himself. And they parted with an unusually deep kiss.

But after that, Thom's communications—mostly emailed by then—became more emotional and insistent. He was asking for something, Perry knew, that was damn near impossible. In order to sort out his own feelings, Perry started doing what he hadn't done in years: he wrote a story. The characters had other names, but they were clearly him and Thom. It was only when he had to come up with an ending that he laid the story aside, carefully hiding the unfinished manuscript.

The next time Thom let him know he'd be in Florida, Perry sent a transparently shaky reason why they wouldn't be able to meet.

Perry, Thom emailed back, *there's a movie I think you should see. It's called* Brokeback Mountain.

Perry didn't want to tell Thom that he'd already seen it. Encroaching suburban sprawl had thrown up a mall with multiplex about twenty miles away, and one Saturday night he and Carrie had left Lisa Marie with a sitter and gone for a rare night out. On the way, Carrie had talked him into seeing *Brokeback Mountain.* "You ain't prejudiced, are you?" she'd semi-taunted, adding that the film was up for an Oscar, unlike the action-picture crap that was also showing at the theater.

Perry couldn't figure out how to get out of seeing the movie without arousing suspicion. And besides, he'd wanted to see it—by himself. He'd thought it was a good movie, real good, though he'd just grunted when Carrie, her face still flushed from tears, asked how he'd liked it. Truth to tell, he wasn't sure why Thom had told him to see it. Sure, it was beautiful—it took place in the country, but it was magnificent country, not flat and boring like shit-ass Florida. And sure, there was the sexual thrill of seeing two improbably handsome cowboys going at it onscreen. But its conventionally downbeat view of the consequences of homosexual lust was hardly an inducement for Perry to leave his increasingly shaky marriage and move out to the City of Angels and shack up with Thom.

He did try to write an ending to his story, though, working on it when Carrie wasn't around. But afterward, instead of hiding the scrawled pages well, he just left them sitting under the socks in his drawer. Not altogether surprisingly, Carrie ran across the story and later confronted her husband, crying, telling him she'd suspected for years. She hadn't, apparently, suggested that they see the movie together just because she liked good tearjerkers.

Perry had phoned Thom to tell him that he and Carrie were calling it quits, and Thom had said he could make it to Florida in a couple of weeks. Having flown all the way from California, Thom was jet-lagged and cranky by the time he maneuvered his rental car into Perry's driveway.

"Carrie?" Thom asked, after they'd shared a joint.

"Moved back with her parents."

"Jesus, I'm sorry."

"Shit happens," Perry said.

"Still."

"So what now?"

"Well, my fucking job is shaky. Looks like the guy who owns the stable is going to sell it. His marriage broke up, too. He needs the money for child support."

"Fuck. Child support."

"Yeah, tell me. But I figured this might be a good opportunity to finally go out to the West Coast."

"Perry..."

"Yeah?"

"I'm living with someone now. A session guitarist. He's a good guy. I'd think you'd like him."

Perry's voice sounded only slightly strained. "Just my fucking luck. How long this been going on?"

"He moved in about a year ago."

"Since before I fucked you?"

"No, after."

"Well."

"Well what?" Thom had cut his hair real short. He looked suddenly middle-aged.

"Can I fuck you again?"

"Don't think so. How's about we go back to the regular?"

That night was the first time Perry ever got rimmed, Thom's tongue licking, teasing, and coaxing open his hole. Maybe it was something his new boyfriend had taught him.

After eating his ass, Thom fucked Perry a good long time, pulling his cock out at the last minute, tearing off the condom, and shooting all over Perry's face. After they wiped up, they fell heavily asleep in each other's arms, both of them knowing this would be final, that something had decisively ended.

In the morning, seeing Thom off on his way to a motel, Perry reached into his desk and pulled out the story he had written, finished at last. Thom started to read it.

"Not now," Perry said. "Not till you get on the plane."

The stable indeed got sold. But Perry's boss put in a good word with some folks he knew, and Perry got hired by Walt Disney World to take care of the horses in Frontierland, and, when he wasn't doing that, to dispatch the trains on the Big Thunder Mountain Railroad ride.

Soon enough, he fell in love with one of the young cast members, a handsome, nicely hung guy who paraded around Fantasyland all day wearing an oversized animal-head mask. Though Perry was maybe happier, in some ways, than he'd ever been, he still missed the open country, flat as it was. He'd drive back north, but the place he grew up in was being transformed into strip malls and retirement communities. There was even a sushi joint one town over. First chance they got, he and Gary took a vacation in the Rockies, the first real mountains Perry had ever seen. On that trip, Perry truthfully didn't think of Thom once.

Carrie found another husband, a bank clerk, so Perry stopped paying child support. He was able to buy a little condo with Gary, and they ended up on the outskirts of Orlando, not far from I-95. They bought the DVD of *Brokeback Mountain* at Wal-Mart, but they never did watch it very much.

RIVER BOY

Tom Cardamone

The town was small and dead and as withered and dry and unwanted as the skeletal, sun-cooked roadkill rattled by the tourists in huge cars who blithely sped by. Armadillos shuffled down Main Street. Main Street was really just the highway that bridged Florida's glittering coasts, spanning mostly farmland and swamp. Arcadia was a few empty storefronts and a courthouse slowly being consumed by dark oaks weary with Spanish moss.

The few citizens of Arcadia lived far from town and far from each other. Everyone was fine with that.

River Boy lived in his grandpa's shack even further from town, close to the river. His grandpa was the forgotten groundskeeper of a forgotten cemetery and had left one morning to hunt deer for their weekly venison stew and never returned. River Boy was fine with that. Not that he didn't love Grandpa—he did, but the man was very old and better to die in the woods and be eaten by foxes than in a hospital in a strange city, life siphoned away by tubes and a wall-mounted television. That had been his grandpa's often-expressed fear.

River Boy had different fears.

He did not tend the graveyard in his grandpa's stead. And so the swamp slowly, methodically absorbed sacred ground with creeping vine and blinking lizard. Some graves were so old that they were marked with nothing more than a pile of resilient shells. This was not a mark of poverty; these oceanic totems possessed the constant hungry whisper of life, to be heard by anyone who happened to pick one up and listen. There was no one to listen. Their white whorls yawned a permanent, stately mourning. This was a graveyard of mostly young men. The town had practically thrown their young at the wars of the world; tall gritty marble obelisks marked the Civil War dead. Smaller, rounded tombstones continued down until the Korean War—not that the town wised up in time for Vietnam, simply they had more or less run out of boys by then. River Boy's father was the only young man to fight and die in Vietnam and he was buried far away. His grandpa did not bring his body home. He said, "He wanted to see the world, so let 'im."

And that was that.

The water of the river was the color of weak tea. Tannin from the decomposing oak leaves strained their moribund blood into the river. The water flowed without hurry. Time between the two coasts slowed, weighed down by the unattended monolithic tombstones of Civil War veterans. Time stalled in the isles of abandoned gas stations, time knotted in leafy coils of kudzu across the pews of empty churches. Time collected in small towns like the brown silt slowly steeping in every bend of the river, rendering River Boy eternally young.

River Boy made his living catching crawdads and selling them to the few families who lived along the river, often trading his catch for fresh milk and eggs and bacon fat. Always shirtless and barefoot, suntanned and lean, his hair a blond bird's nest of tangle and twig, he lived beside the river, near the river, in the river, respectful of the river and its many denizens. He untied sun-drunk coral snakes from atop hot rocks, combed cobwebs from fern and fraternally hugged the sandy clutches of alligator eggs that punctuated the riverbanks. Grandpa had explained that when alligator eggs hatched they were all the same sex, depending upon the temperature during their incubation period. River Boy knew his nurturing embrace rendered the clutch male, and in appreciation the grown gators would allow him to skip across their scaly backs.

And he hid. Hid well. Among the palm fronds and black, heaving roots of ancient cypress; behind waxen walls of rhododendron, River Boy hid. He was always on the lookout, always on guard, against Skink. Skink was mean and Skink was hungry and Skink was forever trying to catch River Boy and force him to the ground and tickle him, the rake of his dirty nails leaving red trails across River Boy's ribs for days afterward. Skink was an older boy; his red hair flamed, angry freckles burrowed into his full cheeks. With his upturned nose River Boy thought he looked like a haughty skunk. Skink was so named because of his freakish ability to scurry up any tree, like the black, rainbow-striped lizard of the same name. Lightning fast, Skink could outrun a wild boar. He liked to drop from a branch onto an unsuspecting River Boy, tickling him until tears ran down his face. He tickled, though lately his hands had begun to claim more from River Boy than he was willing to give.

So River Boy moved quietly through the swamp, deftly lifting stones to catch crawdads. Hoisting them by their red tails to avoid their claws, he dropped them into his battered bait bucket. The swamp was a hot place and the river a ribbon of coolness winding within; River Boy waded the water in threadbare cut-offs, held together by patches and sweat and a rope belt tied tight against a broken zipper gnawing on a wonderful, flaxen weave of pubic hair.

As he rounded a bend he saw Skink. Skink was standing on a huge oak log carpeted with vivid moss, filthy black overalls at his ankles, hands behind his head as he triumphantly pissed a golden arch. River Boy watched as the strong liquid thread hit the water and dissolved into a yellow current wrapping around his knees.

Skink smirked. Looking at River Boy, he licked his white, crooked teeth and flexed his ample biceps, humorously humongous muscles inflated by constant farmwork. The rank hair burning his armpits was matted to his flesh like tree bark by sweat. Concentrating on the arc of his urine, he looked into River Boy's eyes.

"Take a drink."

River Boy knew to obey. To disobey meant being tickled. Wicked fingers would torture his ribs until he lost breath, nearly lost consciousness, and the next day every movement would reverberate throughout his bruised midriff. He approached the liquid rainbow, fearful mouth open. Skink twisted his hips to meet River Boy, his taut stomach flexing as piss flowed through the noose of foreskin at the end of his long prick; curls of orange pubic hair protected furious testicles ready to burst. River Boy stepped into the sun shower; acidic urine washed his lips and burned his gums. He surrendered to the warmth spiraling down his throat and held his arms out in supplication. Skink grinned wickedly and pulled on his rising cock, breaking his stream of piss into rude splashes, painting River Boy's cheeks and stinging his eyes. River Boy plunged into the cleansing water of the river, replacing one baptism with another. He rose and shook the hair out of his face.

Skink kicked off his overalls and crouched on the log, dirty
knees far apart. The shadow of his erection wavered like a bird
of prey upon the water's surface. He smiled a silent command.
River Boy approached, moist lips parted. Suddenly Skink leapt
acrobatically from his roost and in a quick midair somersault
presented his rear instead. He leaned forward and stretched his
arms toward shore, cracking his ass wide open, its dull pink coil
harassed by a mass of wiry crimson. River Boy hesitated. Cool
water lapped at the sinewy knot of his belly button; the current
tugged at his soaked cut-offs, heavy in the water. He'd forgotten about the bait bucket; it had drifted free of his grip and
overturned on a spread of sand on the other side of the river.
Relieved crawdads shambled into the water, looking for new
rocks to crawl under.

He put two wet hands on Skink's asscheeks and spread them
further apart. Skink groaned in anticipation, the pucker of his
ass quivering. River Boy sniffed and momentarily turned away
from the raw mammalian stench, the compost of sweat and
muscle, similar to the scent of decay that pervaded the swamp,
minus the secret sweetness of far-off, never-glimpsed gardenias.
He cupped his hand into the river, then let the coolness cascade
slowly onto Skink's exposed rear. Skink shivered impatiently as
River Boy leaned in, his tongue cleaving Skink's opening. Skink
bucked and pushed his backside roughly into River Boy's face,
gripping the boy's tongue with a mean suction. River Boy stead-
ied himself, hands against grimy log, feet hard on silky sand. He
sucked and lapped at the welcoming hole. Pleasure widened and
internal mucus relaxed the opening as the boy's tongue probed
and Skink growled approval.

Skink pushed River Boy away roughly with the bottom of
his foot and then twisted his body back around. Feet now in
the air, saliva-soaked buttocks skinned black grime off the log,

spreading muck onto his thighs, spackling his rolling testicles. Skink handled his cock. He pulled back pink foreskin to reveal a strong, polished walnut, hard and shiny. River Boy eagerly lapped at the head and gripped the vein-ridden shaft, eyes wide and clear, hoping to penetrate Skink's lustful, commanding stare. Skink positioned himself low, to River Boy's disadvantage. Rather than catching Skink's cock and funneling the shaft down his throat, River Boy found it rocketing against the roof of his mouth, eliciting tears. Skink's eyes narrowed. He pumped his hips with a laconic rhythm and surveyed the river as if he were a satiated alligator, River Boy's open mouth his private grotto. Skink slowed his motion; his saliva-slicked cock popped out from between his servant's full lips. River Boy used the lull to work his way out of his damp cut-offs and toss them up into the grass. He ran his hands over his cold, emancipated buttocks; his nipples were hard and begged for attention but he knew enough not to make any requests, to remain silent until the older boy had had his way and to be grateful if he were then, and only then, allowed to orgasm.

Skink stood suddenly. His fists slung like scythes as he planted his feet wide apart. He caught his wagging cock with one hand and began to pump.

"Suck my balls, River Boy."

He obeyed, crawling across the log and onto the patch of sand and grass Skink had commandeered. River Boy curled his legs at Skink's feet and placed his head reverentially beneath his sac and lapped away. Lips parted, he tried to catch the furry apples in his mouth as they bobbed up and down in rhythm with Skink's forceful jacking. He toyed discreetly with his own burgeoning cock. Tears of milky semen bubbled at the tip. Skink stopped all motion and stepped back with one foot.

River Boy rolled onto his chest and stomach and pulled his

knees up under him. One cheek smooth against the sun-warmed sand, he looked out at the calm flow of the river; cattails waved politely upstream. He relinquished all control and Skink, stomping behind him, spat furiously at his upraised ass. And Skink swore, he said horrible things that River Boy knew were curse words, but they didn't connect together, didn't make sense. Gobs of spit hit the back of his neck, landed between his shoulder blades and slid slowly down. With each bullet of spit Skink swore. His voice grew deeper and when he started quoting the Bible he roared like a black bear.

And with scripture came more spit.

Slugs of saliva wept down the crack of River Boy's ass; he contracted his anus at just the right moment to deliberately draw moisture in. Eyes closed, he imagined he was a giant fragile orchid, white petals unpeeled, his dark ruby center breathing in the rain. He opened his eyes as a row of ants crossed his upturned palm.

Skink marched off into the woods and cut himself a switch. He swore a long, meaningless guttural curse, a war cry. He denuded the branch of leaves and whipped River Boy's flanks. River Boy did not flinch—that would only invite more pain. He closed his eyes again and pretended that the rain was coming down harder now, slicing the white petals, penetrating drops shredding the flower, pushing through to form a wonderful river scented by slaughter. Skink paused to examine the pink cross-stitching of welts rising off of River Boy's buttocks.

River Boy felt a sharpness at his opening and instinctively clenched himself closed. New pain. Resistance and then horrible surrender as Skink pushed more and more of the stick into River Boy. And River Boy cried out at this new intrusion, one leg twitching in revulsion. Immediate withdrawal. River Boy heard the stick revolve through the air and crash into some distant palm fronds, and Skink crashed into him.

Cock against braised ass, pendulous balls knocking, rough hands steered his shoulders into the ground, forcing the wind out of him; River Boy collapsed as Skink rode him hard, bucking wildly. Hollowed out, memories left him, words left him, his own name disappeared as River Boy unfolded, became sand. Cock burrowed boy. Skink unwound into a massive oak and pushed his roots into River Boy, filling each soft vein with probing, angry, coarse wood. River Boy clutched at the sand, grasped at nothing, opened his mouth to scream but nothing came out, and looked up as a long white heron streaked across the sky. He came and Skink came. Skink punched his buttocks, pushed rough, calloused hands into the welts on his ass, kneaded flesh into something shaped only by pain as his cock fired strings of semen into the hole that was River Boy.

Skink pushed himself out and fell backward. Heaving, while he regained control of his breath, he observed River Boy, who rolled onto his back and tried to remember who and where he was. As he stood Skink's vengeful penis retreated into its puckery noose. Towering over River Boy, with his big toe he swirled the droplets of the boy's semen harshly onto his sand-specked stomach.

"You'ns were bad. You'ns need to be punished."

He turned his freckled back to River Boy and walked to the water.

"Next time, I'm takin' you to the Black Shack."

And so River Boy spent his days hunting crawdads, gently giving his warmth to any clutch of alligator eggs he happened upon, all the while moving through the glade like a startled fawn, ever wary that a predator in soiled overalls lurked among the trees.

He was surprised when one morning the predator knocked on his door.

Skink presented himself, freshly bathed and hair combed, in front of River Boy's shack, with a handful of freshly-picked strawberries and a quart of milk. Shocked, River Boy forgot to invite his caller in, but merely sat on the edge of his bed, slack-jawed, rubbing his eyes. The milk obviously came from Skink's family farm. The strawberries were another thing; they only grew in one sunny patch far from town and were considered such a choice delicacy by the large black snakes that sunned themselves there that no one bothered to pick them. River Boy tried to gauge Skink's mood, and started to lower himself to his knees, but the other boy caught him by the elbow and led him to the graveyard. There they picnicked on the tomb of the highest-ranking Civil War soldier they could find.

They spent a quiet morning by the river. River Boy showed Skink how he caught crawdads, that if he turned over a rock and thought the crawdad was too young to be caught, he would say "'cuse me," and politely turn the rock back over. When Skink went to pee he did so discreetly behind a twisted oak. At the sound of him urinating River Boy found himself both relieved and thirsty.

By noon the day was brilliant with heat and River Boy decided to go back home. Skink accompanied him but took his hand when they entered the cemetery. River Boy blushed and felt he was being courted, though he worried that his paramour's earlier threat of punishment might consist of a broken heart rather than a battered rear or bruised ribs. He pulled away but Skink stepped in front of him; the worn strap of his overalls slipped down his shoulder to reveal a pink nipple serrated with pale, sugary goose bumps hemmed by reddish-blond curls.

"Waitaminute."

And with a firm tenderness he took him by the hand and led him to the nearest tombstone. He cleared it of moss and

black lizards and patted it quaintly, invitingly. River Boy sat.
The rough stone felt cool on the backs of his legs.

"I got this for you."

Skink fished a handkerchief out of his back pocket before
sitting down.

River Boy took the handkerchief in both hands. It was light
but somehow felt potent. Skink sat so close River Boy could feel
the warmth of his breath.

"Open it." The command was gentle, the look in Skink's blue
eyes sincere. Today was the first day River Boy was able to see
the color of his eyes. He unfolded the cloth and felt a mixture of
concern and disappointment.

Whatever he might have anticipated, this was not it.

The limp mushroom was a grayish brown and had been com-
pressed into further lifelessness from its time in Skink's pocket.

"Eat it."

That was the last thing River Boy wanted to do. Grandpa
had taught him so much, but had not had time to teach him everything. River Boy didn't know which mushrooms were good
and which ones were bad. The bad ones were like a snakebite:
first you're paralyzed, then your throat constricts, then you die.
And it takes hours to die. Clouds passed between the sun and the
cemetery and everything darkened. The solemn tombs blended
with low branches thick with vine.

"G'wan. Eat it." Skink blinked. His azure eyes sparkled.
River Boy thought about that morning when his grandpa left to
go hunting. He shut the door behind him and never came back.

He put the tiny mushroom in his mouth and chewed. It had
the texture of beef but no flavor. The aftertaste was similar to
cold semen but with an added heaviness, a lingering lifelessness
that filled River Boy with regret.

Skink uncharacteristically patted River Boy's thigh, rushed to the well, vigorously pumped the handle and filled his hand with cool water. He stepped lightly so little was spilt and let River Boy lap his hand clean. Refreshed, he stretched out on the grave and rested his head in Skink's lap. Skink ran his fingers slowly through River Boy's hair. They watched the breeze calmly sweep through the trees. As the clouds passed the sun sparkled off the Formica embedded in some nearby tombstones.

And then the sparkles danced and spun and shot through the trees like wild stars. River Boy was giddy and started to clap. His cheeks were flushed. His toes and fingers tingled. When he looked at Skink he was surprised to see that he looked younger, his hair seemed longer, leaves and buds curled and slithered, hidden among the locks. One bud opened to display a tiny row of red, needle-like teeth. It hissed at him.

River Boy shot out of Skink's lap and spun around. The graveyard suddenly stretched for miles, tombs were silently consumed by the earth while others rose like Aztec pyramids to block out the sun.

A caring hand fell lightly on his shoulder.

"Hey. It's all right. It's going to be all right."

Scared, River Boy turned to look at Skink. Skink smiled, his hair was normal, blazing happily in the sunlight. He put both hands on the boy's shoulders.

"It's all right. I just wanted to show you the Black Shack."

So everything wasn't all right, he thought. Skink had a new room in which to torture him, the mushroom was its key.

The hands on his shoulders felt reassuring, though. He looked deep into Skink's eyes.

And saw the river.

The river flowed, leaves spun on the surface. Everything went in the same direction.

"There." Skink's voice had an echo. "There's the Black Shack."

He spun River Boy around to face his own home. The small wooden lean-to was exactly the same: corrugated tin roof aslant a jumble of poorly nailed boards.

Except the door was open, and he had left it closed.

Darkness emanated from within.

Skink urged him onward with a friendly shove. The walk toward his strange home had lengthened; the surrounding swamp was an alien jungle. Atop one tombstone a two-headed heron fought itself over a torn crawdad dripping between its dueling beaks. River Boy paused at the doorway. He thought of knocking, laughed and stepped in.

The artificial feeling of elation left him. Light no longer seemed like it might leap away. The misperception of distance and depth evaporated. He was in his comfortable little home shrouded in midday shadows while a crowd of dusty motes pleasantly floated about.

And then he saw himself, twisted among the sheets of his bed.

River Boy saw himself as Skink must see him: lithe and tan and beautiful, filled with a palpable innocence that ignited a certain craving, a craving he felt himself. His cock engorged with fraternal lust as his double rolled on the bed.

He admired his ankles, strong yet fawnlike, shaded with light curls.

He admired the slight musculature of his lean, tanned thighs.

The double flailed slightly in his deep sleep, casting aside the sheet.

He admired his cock, the brown flesh of his testicles pulled taut by a wavering wand anointed with crystalline drops of semen.

Their twin cocks twitched in unison.

He wanted to reach out and stroke his chest. His acorn nipples perked at the idea.

He tilted his head; he had never noticed that his dark lashes were so long. When closed, his dreamer's face seemed so peaceful, as if a river flowed beneath it.

He admired his parted lips, red and cracked from night-thirst.

Hastily unfastened jean shorts dropped to the floor.

River Boy dove onto the previously unvanquished bed.

He grappled with his sleeping double. The twin moaned, his eyelids fluttered, but he did not speak or open his eyes. Feet interlocked like kudzu. Fingers grasped wrists. His double parted his legs beneath the rough thrusting and lifted his knees. River Boy planted his cock at his own ass and paused to allow the leakage of semen to swab a semblance of lubrication. The head of his cock nestled against the pink divide; he marveled at the grip and feel of his own ass. He was both beggar and coin. Moistened with sweat and hunger, it palpitated and seemed to reach for the cock at its bay.

River Boy wondered which of the two was the dreamer.

And he rode and he shivered as dual sensation rocked both bodies. Internal storms. Eyes closed, sparks of light twirled and danced. There was a wind that roared through the world as his cock slipped in and out of his own wanton vortex.

He kissed himself and realized that this was his first kiss.

Motion subsided slightly as he looked toward the door and thought of Skink behind it.

Skink should be his first kiss.

Skink *would* be his first kiss.

It's not what happens inside the Black Shack, he thought, *it's what happens outside that matters.*

Realization bloomed harder and faster than a kiss. He wrapped his tongue around his double's tongue and straightened his legs and let go of everything, and gravity failed and he launched milky comets and stars into himself and he felt the riddle of his spine unwind and course like molten wax down his ribs to fuse around his heart, his twin hearts, their double-beat stopped.

And restarted, breaking their wax casing into a thousand shards of rotting orchid petals.

Even pulling out of himself was an internal cascade of sparks. Both gasped. His double opened his eyes.

They looked into each other's eyes.

Into the deepest part of the river.

Swirling pupils the centers of which are where water divides.

They separated there, hands loosened their grip to float free as autumnal leaves, leaves that tossed by the current appeared to slowly wave good-bye.

Or hello.

"Hello."

Skink smiled and pressed the back of his hand to River Boy's forehead.

River Boy sat on the edge of the bed. The door was wide open, framing a blue sky and dark tree limbs. River Boy was tired and Skink was concerned. He helped River Boy rise and walk outside. The ground felt new and particular beneath River Boy's feet. He felt the impression of every single grain of sand and was grateful for this new insight. His fingers grazed the rough cornices of tombstones as he passed through the cemetery and he shivered at the stories they told. He noticed a peculiar inscription on a nameless slab of marble he'd not noticed before: *The renewal of wonderment is as grand as it is ageless.*

The boys went to the river to cleanse themselves. Skink washed River Boy gently, as the boy quietly examined the canopy above, head cocked at the trill of birdsong. The waters were baptismal and uplifting. Their kiss was a private sunrise. Slowly they danced on the backs of aloof alligators clinging to the cool riverbed.

ABOUT THE AUTHORS

SHANE ALLISON done been called a fag, a nigger an' a genius; his work done graced th' pages of small an' big ol' magazines like *Mississippi Review* an' *New Delta Review*, Suspect Thoughts an' Velvet Mafia, Outsider Ink an' juked, an' some good ol' boy anthologies like *Best Black Gay Erotica* an' *Ultimate Gay Erotica 2006* and *2007*, *Cowboys: Gay Erotic Tales*, *Hustlers* an' *Best Gay Erotica 2007*. He da edita' of *Hot Cops: Gay Erotic Tales*.

STEVE BERMAN is a suburban brat, and the closest he has come to country life is turning the dial on the car radio past honky-tonk stations. That said, he has camped out on the Mongolian steppes, seduced a Kansas teen in a bathtub, and found the time to write a novel, *Vintage, a Ghost Story*, about a few young men haunted by love. For other queer and weird info about Steve and his many published stories, visit his site, www.steveberman.com.

MICHAEL BRACKEN, a Derringer Award-winning mystery writer, is the author of eleven books, including *All White Girls* and *Yesterday in Blood and Bone*, and more than one thousand shorter works that have appeared in literary, small press, and commercial publications worldwide. Bracken is also the editor of eight published or forthcoming crime fiction anthologies.

TOM CARDAMONE is the author of the erotic novel *The Werewolves of Central Park*. He has several projects, fiction and nonfiction, on the horizon. Read some of his short, sharp, speculative fiction at his website, www.pumpkinteeth.net.

DALE CHASE has been writing male erotica for eight years, with more than one hundred stories published in various magazines and anthologies, including translation into German. Her first literary effort was published in *The Harrington Gay Men's Fiction Quarterly*. *The Company He Keeps*, her collection of Victorian gentlemen's erotica, is due in 2007. Chase lives near San Francisco and is currently at work on a collection of ghostly male erotica.

KAL COBALT was born and raised in a small Oregon town where the diner across the street from the railroad depot was always open. See more work in *Hot Gay Erotica*, *Best Fantastic Erotica*, *Distant Horizons* and at www.kalcobalt.com.

WAYNE COURTOIS, a country boy from Maine who now lives in Kansas City, is author of the novels *My Name Is Rand* and the forthcoming *A Pardoner's Tale*. His fiction has appeared in the webzines Suspect Thoughts and Velvet Mafia, in *Harrington Gay Men's Fiction Quarterly*, and in anthologies such as *Of the Flesh*, *Love Under Foot*, *Best Gay Erotica 2005*, *Out of Control* and *Hot Gay Erotica*. Visit him at www.waynecourtois.com.

VINCENT DIAMOND is a Florida writer with stories in *Best Gay Love Stories 2005*, *Best Gay Love Stories 2006*, *Feathers*, *Play Ball*, *Men of Mystery: Tales of Erotica and Suspense*, *Best Gay Romance 2007* and *Truckers*. Diamond gleefully buys smutty periodicals for "research materials" and lists them on a Schedule C every year. The IRS has yet to question this deduction. Contact: www.vincentdiamond.com.

JACK FRITSCHER: Fifty years as published author; seventeen books; four hundred articles/stories, one thousand photographs in thirty-eight magazines; writer-director, one hundred sixty-two homomasculine videos: www.PalmDriveVideo.com; author of world's first PhD dissertation on Tennessee Williams (1967), 1968 novel *I Am Curious (Leather)* [*Leather Blues*]; founding San Francisco editor, *Drummer* magazine. Books: memoir-bio of his bi-coastal lover, *Mapplethorpe: Assault with a Deadly Camera*; *Popular Witchcraft* (1972 and 2005); and Lambda Award-nominee, *Some Dance to Remember: A Memoir-Novel of 18th and Castro 1970-1982*. "Gay Heritage" research: www.JackFritscher.com.

JAY NEAL was born and raised in Kansas and knows more about parts of it than he would have chosen to. Having gone to college in Iowa, he's developed a keen appreciation for corn-fed country boys and their big farm equipment. Forsaking rural life for the Washington, DC suburbs years ago, he now only fantasizes—and then writes—about sex on the Great Plains. Current information is at his website: http://bearcastle.com/jayneal.

C. B. POTTS loves the woods, but spends most of her time navigating the wilderness of her office. The author of *Tuesday's*

Rubies and the forthcoming *The Rockhound's Riddle*, she also has stories in Cleis's *Hot Gay Erotica*, *Truckers* and *Cowboys: Gay Erotic Tales*. You can find out more at www.cbpotts.net.

DOMINIC SANTI is a former technical editor turned rogue whose dirty stories have appeared in many dozens of anthologies and magazines, including *Best American Erotica*, several volumes of *Best Gay Erotica* (including 2007), *Second Skins*, *Secret Slaves* and *His Underwear*. Santi's latest solo book is the German collection *Kerle im Lustrausch* (*Horny Guys*). Forthcoming plans include many more short stories, a heretical novel, and another long vacation.

SIMON SHEPPARD is the author of *In Deep: Erotic Stories*, *Kinkorama*, *Sex Parties 101*, and the award-winning *Hotter Than Hell*. He's also coedited *Rough Stuff* and *Roughed Up* and is the editor of the forthcoming *Homosex: Sixty Years of Gay Erotica*. His work appears in over two hundred anthologies, including many editions of *Best Gay Erotica* and *The Best American Erotica*. He writes the syndicated column "Sex Talk," lives queerly in San Francisco, and hangs out at www.simon-sheppard.com. He can't quit you...

J. M. SNYDER is a self-published author of gay erotica whose short fiction appears online at various erotic journals, such as Ruthie's Club and Sticky Pen. His novella *Trin* is available electronically from Aspen Mountain Press, and he is the author of the novels *Vince*, *Power Play*, *Operation Starseed*, *Stepping Up to the Plate* and *It's All Relative*, and the short-story collections *Shorts* and *Bones of the Sea*. For more information, including fiction, excerpts, purchasing details, and updates, please visit www.jmsnyder.net.

KARL TAGGART abhors the current based-on-a-true-story trend in fiction but admits that some of his country encounter actually happened and leaves it to the reader to decide which part. Karl has been writing erotica for a number of years for both magazines and anthologies while working a day job at an insurance company. They have no idea a porn writer lurks in their midst. Karl loves his motorcycle almost as much as his men and is thrilled when he can combine the two.

DUANE WILLIAMS lives in Hamilton, Canada. His short fiction has appeared widely in anthologies, including *Quickies, Queer View Mirror I & II*, Blithe House, *Boyfriends from Hell*, Velvet Mafia, Suspect Thoughts, *Buttmen 2 & 3, Harrington Gay Men's Literary Quarterly, Friction 6, Between the Palms: A Collection of Gay Travel Erotica, Latin Boys, Full Body Contact, Best Gay Erotica 2006* and *Ultimate Gay Erotica 2007*. He can be reached at duanewilliams@cogeco.ca.

ABOUT THE EDITOR

RICHARD LABONTÉ lives some of the time in a wee Perth, Ontario apartment, and some of the time in a sprawling ten-bedroom farmhouse on two hundred acres of land near Calabogie, Ontario that he bought thirty years ago with a crew of college-era friends who lived together in co-op households between 1969 and 1979. From 1979 to 2000, he helped found and then manage A Different Light Bookstores in Los Angeles, New York, West Hollywood, and San Francisco. He has edited the *Best Gay Erotica* series since 1997; coedited *The Future is Queer* (Arsenal Pulp Press, 2006) with Lawrence Schimel; reviews one hundred books a year for Q Syndicate, which distributes his fortnightly column, "Book Marks"; writes the sort-of-monthly subscription newsletter *Books to Watch Out For/Gay Men's Edition;* writes book reviews for *Publishers Weekly*; and, to make a living, edits technical writing. He lives with his husband Asa, who moved to the Canadian countryside from the big city of San Francisco, but confesses that he occasionally misses the concrete. Contact: tattyhill@gmail.com.